Silence in a World Full of Thunder

Rachel Karrington

ARCHWAY
PUBLISHING

This is a work of fiction. All of the characters, names, incidents, organizations, and dialogue in this novel are either the products of the author's imagination or are used fictitiously.

Archway Publishing books may be ordered through booksellers or by contacting:

Archway Publishing
1663 Liberty Drive
Bloomington, IN 47403
www.archwaypublishing.com
1 (888) 242-5904

ISBN: 978-1-4808-4047-8 (sc)
ISBN: 978-1-4808-4048-5 (e)

Library of Congress Control Number: 2016919498

Print information available on the last page.

Archway Publishing rev. date: 12/9/2016

1

Sixteen-year-old Kanasia and her mother, Samantha, lived in a first-floor apartment of a two-family home. They rented from the Odamn family, who were friends from church. Her mother thought it was a good move because it was in a better neighborhood and in the suburbs of Mount Carmel, Illinois. The house had heat, water, and hardwood floors. It was neat and clean, in a great location for taking public transportation. They had beautiful antique furniture and a television and stereo to fill every bedroom. Best of all, they would be renting from some sanctified born-again believers whom they'd known for at least sixteen years from their church. Samantha and Kanasia had eagerly anticipated life in their new home. Little did they know moving into that house would be like relocating to hell.

Kanasia's mother was loving, friendly, caring, generous, and always willing to help someone less fortunate than she, and she was a praying Christian woman. Samantha had a great eye for fashion, decorating, and choosing the best ceramics, crystal vases, flutes, paintings, and antiques. She didn't bother anyone or overstay her welcome, and she had plenty of friends in and outside the church. Samantha didn't hesitate to speak her mind and put folks in their places when they overstepped their boundaries. She loved her telephone and called her friends and family daily. And now she and her daughter had a nice safe place to live. At least that's how it seemed in the beginning.

The landlord's name was Ronald. He, his wife, and their four children were friendly and helpful. He was a carpenter by trade and a hardworking family man. Eventually, his hard work had paid off, and he'd bought his first house. He was also able to buy his first new car, a red two-door Pacer. The car was so small that Ronald had to make two trips to take the four children places.

Their house was minimally equipped with what some would consider necessities. They had few pieces of furniture and no telephone, fan, air conditioner, stereo, or radio. The family did have a television though.

Many would consider the family dysfunctional. At least it didn't seem to be like other families Kanasia knew. The wife, Bey, never cooked for Ronald; the two eldest daughters cooked for him. There also seemed to be a lot of fighting between the parents. Rolanda, their eldest daughter, and Kanasia were good friends. Both attended the same Sunday school class and were junior choir members in the church. One time Rolanda told Kanasia that her father had a fight with her mother and threw a plate at her face. It hit her, causing a cut by the crease of her lips that extended to her cheek. It left a horrible scar resembling a pumpkin carving for Halloween. Rolanda also mentioned that her mother and father slept in different bedrooms. There was always a cold silence when in the presence of Ronald and Bey.

At first, Ronald and Bey were friendly to Kanasia and her mother. But little by little, their characters changed. The friendly conversations, laughs, and smiles were soon gone. The happiness Kanasia and her mother felt when they first moved into their new home turned into disappointment, deception, and misery. They were not allowed to use the backyard or their air conditioner.

Kanasia and Samantha stopped receiving their mail. The utility company threatened to shut off their electricity because Samantha had not paid the bill. Before long, Samantha's phone was disconnected for no payment. Samantha told the telephone company she'd never received a bill from November to April, but the telephone company told her the bills had been sent to the new address. In other words, they didn't believe her.

The Odamn family made their lives a living hell. They seemed to be jealous about Samantha and Kanasia's resources, and they showed it through harassment and hatred. Samantha discovered that Bey and the children were taking their mail. Then Ronald increased their rent, and he complained about noise or claimed he could smell cigarette smoke coming from the apartment. He and Bey began asking Samantha if she was doing hoodoo.

The harassment got to be too much. Samantha went to a city rent control mediator to ask if they could raise her rent after just six months. The mediator told her the increase was illegal and in violation of the rental contract. When Samantha confronted Ronald about the rent increase, he told her, "If you don't pay the increased amount, you'll be evicted from here."

Samantha began to pray and search for a place to move. She was stressed by the ongoing harassment and lack of freedom to live in peace. Every day Ronald accused her of using hoodoo, in an attempt to ruin her reputation as a devout Christian woman. Upset, Samantha always told him to stop, rebuked him in the name of Jesus, and slammed the door in his face. Ronald seemed to prey on them because Samantha and Kanasia did not have a man in their household.

One of the ministers affiliated with Samantha and Kanasia's old church had opened a new one around the corner from their apartment, and there was a guest speaker on the night of July 18, 1981. This minister was well known in the religious community for being "on fire for God." They wanted to hear him preach.

In church, Kanasia saw her mother change physically and mentally. Samantha started babbling and mumbling. She couldn't understand what her mother was saying—or trying to say. Samantha's eyes drifted as if she was confused or dizzy.

She kept turning her head from side to side as if trying to keep her neck from stiffening. Then Samantha went up to the altar and asked the minister to pray for her children. He refused, saying, "Your children need to pray for themselves!"

Samantha was so disappointed and frustrated that they left immediately, not waiting for the service to end. Samantha walked unsteadily on the way home from church. Kanasia grabbed her by the arm several times to prevent her from falling or tripping.

Once home, Samantha lay on her bed talking on the phone with her best friend, Lollie, about her disappointment with the minister that night. Suddenly, she fell off the bed.

Kanasia ran over to her and helped her mother up from the floor. Kanasia was increasingly frightened as she watched her mother become more incoherent and continue to mumble. She screamed, "Mom, what's happening to you?" Tears rolled down Kanasia's face. The house was so hot that Kanasia, Samantha, and Samantha's four grandchildren slept on a quilt on the floor of the living room. She hoped it was a bad nightmare and her mother would be better after they slept. Samantha laid on the living room floor too but at the end next to their piano.

The kids slept quietly through the night, but Kanasia was worried. Samantha tried to get up to go to the bathroom, but she couldn't. She fell and hit the right side of her head on the piano. Kanasia saw the bright red blood run from her mother's head to the floor and ran to help her. Samantha was talking, but Kanasia couldn't understand what she was saying. Kanasia was so afraid; her heart pounded and felt as if it were going to jump from her chest with each beat. The commotion woke up the children. Kanasia ran to the telephone and called 911. She then called her two brothers, Orain and Eddie, to tell them something was wrong with their mother.

Orain and Eddie arrived just before the ambulance. After a quick examination, attendants put Samantha in the ambulance and took her to the local hospital for further evaluation. Kanasia was terrified as they sat and waited to find out what happened to their mother. After three hours, doctors came out and told Kanasia, Orain, and Eddie that their mother had a stroke. Her left side was paralyzed. Kanasia's heart beat like a drummer striking his instruments with his sticks. She was frightened and nervous; she didn't know what to do or think. They called their other siblings to tell them about Samantha. They also got in touch with the Red Cross to notify their brother Rick, who was in the military, to come home.

After Samantha was admitted to the hospital, her family was allowed to go back to see her. She lay there moaning, mumbling, confused, and combative. It was a scary sight for all of them.

Rick arrived from the Philippines two days later. He was so distraught after seeing their mother that he went to Ronald's apartment and pounded on the door. He confronted Ronald and his family, accusing them of causing

Samantha's stroke. The landlord shook and had fear in his eyes. Ronald clearly knew that Rick was upset and not playing with him. Even though Ronald denied having anything to do with Samantha's sickness. Kanasia was glad someone confronted Ronald about all the aggravation and harassment they endured.

The situation overwhelmed all of them but especially Kanasia, as she was the last child living at home. *Who's going to take care of me now? Where am I going to stay?* Samantha had always taken care of her. They'd prayed and read Scriptures together. They'd laughed and talked together. They had always been so close and had a great relationship.

As days passed, Samantha became more and more confused instead of getting better. She tried to rip off her clothes. She took swings at everybody, always ready to fight. Kanasia would call out to her, but it didn't matter. Samantha was in her own world.

Her mother's condition and lack of progress made Kanasia depressed. She felt all alone in the world, with no one to protect her. Kanasia cried out, "Lord, what am I going to do?" Her brother consoled her as she sobbed.

While Samantha was in the hospital, Orain began taking over her bills and searching for an apartment for Kanasia and their mother to live in. Orain sold Samantha's car in order to pay the rental agency their finder's fee for finding them an apartment away from those crazy church people's house. Rick assisted with the moving and watched over Kanasia while their mother was in the hospital. The fact that they were finally moving was a great feeling for Kanasia and she could finally sleep at night without all the confusion she had been surrounded by for all those months of living in Ronald's house. They found out the day they were moving that the Odamn family wanted them out so they could rent to another family in the church.

2

⁓

It was now September, and Samantha was still in the hospital. As the days moved forward, she wasn't getting any better. Samantha didn't have health insurance, so the social worker applied for state Medicaid and Medicare insurance so the hospital could be compensated for the medical bills. This was another reason for the extended stay, along with digestion complications that required a feeding tube from her nose to her abdomen.

At first, their plan for her was rehabilitation, but once the feeding tube was placed, rehabilitation was out the door. Then Samantha's doctor had a meeting with the family and told them that she would never walk or even sit up on her own again, because the stroke she had was that bad. The doctor told them to consider placing their mother in a nursing home or taking her home and having a health service provider come out to care for her. Rick ran out of the hospital and began to scream and cry. Kanasia went to console him, and they cried together. They all felt hopeless and discouraged.

On the way home, Kanasia became very angry with God and decided to stop praying and reading her Bible. She now resented the foundation she grew up with and blamed God for all her problems.

The days went so fast, and it was soon time for Rick to go back to his duties with the military. Kanasia had to live alone in the new apartment while Samantha continued to stay at the hospital. Little by little, her speech and alertness began to get better.

Kanasia was in the eleventh grade now and getting ready to attend a new high school. She left Harrington High School, a performance arts school in Mount Carmel, to attend Jackson High School in Jameson, located in the next town over. Living in Jameson was a decision that Samantha and Kanasia made before she got sick, but attending Jackson High School was Orain's idea since he was buying a house in this area. Kanasia had no desire to leave her mother to go to school. But she knew she still had to get her education, not cause any problems, and make her mother proud.

With everything going on, Kanasia had no new school clothes, but thank God no one knew her there so it didn't matter what she wore. One good thing about attending school in the suburbs, where it was predominantly white, was that they weren't into the "got to have new clothes thing" like at a predominantly black school in the hood. This school was mixed with various nationalities, but the Blacks, Asians, and Latinos in the school were definitely the minority among the Caucasians .

Kanasia started to like this new school, guidance counselor, teachers, and she made some friends too. As time went on, she realized this was her escape from dealing with her mother's illness. She began focusing on herself a little. She began to enjoy her new environment, and she really loved the school's curriculum because it was so diverse compared to the performing arts school. She enjoyed being able to choose courses that she had an interest in, and there were so many to courses to venture into.

Come November, Samantha was still in the hospital, but she was beginning to be more alert and was speaking again. It was a pleasure to visit her. On the weekends, Kanasia would get lunch and climb up in the bed with her mother and talk to her, braid her hair, and watch television with her. It was so good to have her mother talking again and making sense. She loved her mother so much, and the thought of losing her in any capacity was devastating.

One day when Kanasia went to see her mother, Samantha asked, "Kanasia, am I going to a nursing home?"

Kanasia was so surprised to hear her say that, because neither Orain nor any of her other siblings had made that decision. "Mom, why would you ask me that?"

She said, "I heard the nurses talking about it yesterday."

She was stunned and didn't know how to respond to her mother. When Kanasia left the hospital later that night, she called Orain and informed him of what their mother had asked her, how she had overheard that from the nursing staff. She felt that their mother's health information was being disclosed in an inappropriate way, especially outside of her hospital room, where she could hear. Oftentimes health-care staff assume that because you're not talking to them, you are deaf or dumb, so they say what they want, even the heartbreaking stuff.

Orain was so upset that he confronted the nurses about talking about their mother right in front of her or outside her room. Orain told the staff, "How dare you discuss this information around our mother when we, as her family, have not even made that decision!" He was hot and red in the face. The nurses were speechless but later came to apologize for their actions.

Weeks passed. It was a few days before Thanksgiving when Samantha finally got health insurance. But despite the health insurance, she was still not a candidate for the rehabilitation programs at the outpatient facilities because of the feeding tube that was still in place. The family had not discussed the nursing home with their mother, because they were hoping the outpatient rehabilitation facility was still an option. So now they were back to only two choices. They had a family meeting to discuss whether to get the health service at home or place their mother in a nursing home for care. The only thing about the home care was that someone besides Kanasia would have to be available to help her care for their mother during the times when she was at school, since Samantha couldn't be left alone.

Her siblings could be so selfish. No one wanted to sacrifice to help Kanasia take care of their mother at home. Kanasia was outvoted, which meant she would have to give up the apartment and go live with one of her brothers and his family. This was very disturbing, and she guessed that nobody wanted her either. Nobody wanted to care for a sixteen-year-old girl or had any confidence in her as a developing young teenager, and her life had been turned upside down due to her mother's illness. All they could think of was going on with their lives uninterrupted. They lacked concern, compassion, love, and understanding. They also thought of the negative things that Kanasia could encounter, such as teenage pregnancy, becoming a prostitute, or drugs. Where was the family unity, foundation, and support that they were taught by their parents?

Kanasia's sister, Paris, was busy trying to become a singer and actress. She was so busy constantly trying to get auditions for commercials and plays that she didn't have the time or money to make the sacrifice. On top of that, she lived in Michigan. She had her own problems going on with her two daughters that she now had to raise because Samantha and Kanasia could no longer do it. Paris was not stable and was always in between boyfriends. There was always some domestic violence involved in her relationships. She told Kanasia that she could live with her, but Kanasia knew that she would automatically become a babysitter and be subjected to the physical and verbal abusive relationships that Paris was involved in with her boyfriends.

Kanasia wasn't about to leave her mother alone either. She knew she was the only true support system that Samantha had. If she left, that would cause her mother to lose all hope of returning home and send her into a deep depression and eventually death.

The decision was finally made, and Kanasia and Orain had to be the ones to tell their mother. They decided to tell Samantha a couple of days before the nursing plans were put into place by the hospital social worker. Tears began to cascade down Kanasia's face, flowing like a waterfall. She dreaded this and didn't want to tell her mother that she would be living at a nursing home, nor did she want to disappoint her. Kanasia knew this was not what Samantha imagined, especially after working in a nursing home as a missionary with the church. Samantha went on Sunday mornings to provide prayer meetings with the residents, singing, and uplifting them spiritually. Kanasia cried and began to cuddle her mother like a baby as Orain told her that she was going to be transferred into a nursing home for further care.

It was finally time to move their mother to the nursing home via ambulance. It was the day before Christmas Eve.

"God, why?" Kanasia cried. "Why do we have to suffer like this after all our prayers, fasting, sacrificing, trusting you, and believing in you?" Kanasia felt so depressed and as if no one gave a damn about them. The only reason she didn't end her life was because she knew her mother needed her most of all.

The only good thing about this nursing home was that it was within walking distance from the new apartment she moved into. This gave her mother some hope that she would eventually be back home with Kanasia. Kanasia visited the nursing home every day so Samantha didn't feel alone. Kanasia kept up her spirits in front of her mother so she wouldn't ruin her mood or upset her.

When Paris came to town to see their mother, they went over to the nursing home to visit. When they approached her room, however, they saw that their mother wasn't there. So they went to the nurses' station to inquire about their mother and where she was. After they'd waited awhile, a nurse finally came to tell them that their mother was transferred back to the hospital because she became sick. Paris and Kanasia were devastated that the staff never reached out to let the family know about their mother being sent back to the hospital.

Paris and Kanasia immediately grabbed a cab to the hospital. They informed Orain and Eddie of their mother's admission to the hospital. This time their mother was admitted to ICU. She had a high fever, her skin was like a light gray, she was gasping for air, and her lips were blue. The nurse placed her on oxygen and hooked her up to all kinds of IV fluids. She wasn't talking, and she looked so weak. The doctors later told the family that their mother had developed pneumonia and would be in the hospital until she recovered.

The holidays were ruined. It was bad enough that Kanasia's mother was no longer living at home, but now they were going back up to the hospital to visit her on Christmas Day. Kanasia was so afraid she was going to lose her. She cried so much that her eyes were red and bloodshot. Insomnia, along with loss of appetite, took over.

It took about two weeks until Samantha was talking again. But unfortunately, that meant it was time for her to go back to the nursing home. It was also time for Paris to go back to Michigan. Once again, Kanasia had to adapt to her new life without her mother, but she took advantage of every opportunity to see her at the nursing home.

Little did her mother know that the nursing home took her whole social security check for her room and board, medications, and treatment plans. All that was left was Kanasia's social security check from her father's death, payments called survivors monthly benefits, which was only $240 per month. This was not enough to pay the rent, utilities, food, and money for her bus card.

Kanasia began searching for jobs to work after school in order to keep the apartment. She was willing to do this to avoid living with any of her brothers or sister. She even went as far as asking if she could live with one of her mother's church friends; Mother Toss, their neighbor Ola, cousin Marge, and even godmother Tina. The only two that were willing to help were Ola and Marge, but they both had dogs and Kanasia wasn't a dog fan. The odor in the air was a raw, dirty, and nauseating stench. She knew that she wouldn't be able to eat or drink in these houses if she had to live there. Deep inside, Kanasia knew they really were afraid to get involved in her family business.

Kanasia went to the social worker at the hospital to get assistance. She didn't even try to help her and thought Kanasia had a problem for not wanting to live with her family. Every option turned into a dead end. Eventually, Kanasia decided to move in with her eldest brother, Eddie, and his family.

It was now January 1982, and their apartment was gone. Kanasia was preparing to move in with Eddie.

"Damn. Damn!" she shouted.

She hated this with a passion and knew her mother or father would never want her to live with Eddie. But she had no choice, as no one else wanted her. Kanasia experienced major depression, loss of appetite, weight loss, anger, disappointment, and hopelessness. Rumbles of sadness erupted inside of her as tears trailed down her face. "I don't deserve this shit!"

Kanasia knew that was the beginning of her downward spiral with verbal, mental, and physical abuse due to Orain's refusal to allow her to live with him and his wife. Kanasia had to walk to school and the nursing home because she had no money for bus fare. She had no lunch money, no new clothes or shoes for school, and no health-care coverage in case she got sick and needed to go to the doctor or hospital. If she got sick, Kanasia would have to try to feel better on her own. She felt so down from all the abuse.

The abuse was imposed upon her because Kanasia was Samantha's baby, the sheltered one, the little princess, and the untouchable one. Eddie yelled at her and criticized her. His sons lied by telling their father Kanasia was cursing in their house. This was the only way they could get her in trouble with their father, and it also entertained them. Due to their lies, she would get thrown up against the wall with Eddie's hands wrapped around her neck, squeezing tightly and cutting off her air. This left Kanasia gasping for breath, shaking like a wavering tree in a violent tornado causing Kanasia out of fear to expel a gush of urine in her panties running down her legs.

"I am not putting up with your shit. Cursing in my house!" screamed Eddie.

Kanasia pleaded, "I didn't curse in your house, and I would never disrespect your house."

Kanasia already knew where she stood with them, so she wouldn't jeopardize her stay there by creating a hostile environment. But Eddie and his family didn't speak Spanish, so Kanasia would vent by cursing in Spanish. She would walk around saying "Bece mi cula!" ("Kiss my ass.")

Kanasia had to de-stress and rebel to their raw, evil treatment in some way to cope with them. But one thing about Eddie was that he was an army veteran with a bad drinking problem, and this was when his boldness and nasty, negative, and judgmental side came out. Eddie's real inner feelings about Kanasia came to the surface.

Orain also took advantage of Kanasia financially by not giving her enough money or no money at all for food, bus fare, from her monthly social security benefits. Because she took the bus to school and went to see their mother at the nursing home, some days the only food Kanasia had was the school breakfast and lunch.

She walked an hour to school every day and two hours from school to visit her mother. On the weekends, it would take her an hour to walk because she came from home. Kanasia hated walking, but if it meant getting an education and seeing her mother to get some peace of mind, she didn't mind. All this walking kept her skinny as hell. Kanasia clothes were hanging off her as if she were sick. She always had to wear a belt to hold up her skirt or pants.

Throughout all the negative atmosphere, she was determined to keep her grades up and maintain honor roll status. She worked hard in school and even took a writing class that allowed her to express herself in writing. Kanasia began to keep a diary, and she wrote an essay on the problems she was having since her mother's stroke. Kanasia's writing teacher, Mrs. Smith, was amazed by her writing skills and encouraged Kanasia to continue writing and do it on a daily basis. Kanasia learned that she loved to write, and it gave her an outlet to relieve the stress she was enduring at Eddie's and with her mother's illness.

No matter how down she felt inside, she always tried to keep her appearances together by wearing makeup and keeping her clothes neat and presentable. But when Eddie drank, he would put Kanasia down and constantly rip her character apart. He would yell at her, "You ain't going to be nothing but pregnant or on drugs! You look like a clown or Minnie Mouse with all that makeup on! She would often cry herself to sleep, and sometimes she couldn't sleep at all. Kanasia was hoping this was just a bad nightmare.

He would also go into her bedroom and complain that she wasn't keeping it clean. Then the yelling would start, followed by the name-calling. Kanasia's eyes were ringed with redness, pockets of swelling surrounded by lines of engraved darkness, starving for lubrication and rest. She wondered what she did to deserve all the abuse.

This time in Kanasia's life made her both furious and depressed. It began a period of self-abuse, and she started cutting her arms. One time she cut her left upper arm so deeply that the blood was running down her arm like a running faucet. Kanasia ran to the bathroom to clean her arm, and she saw Eddie getting ready to go out to the bar for the night. He saw the blood and came with her into the bathroom to help her stop the bleeding.

Eddie said, "What happened? Did you cut yourself?"

Kanasia was so embarrassed. "Yes," she replied.

Kanasia wanted to kill herself to avoid dealing with the abuse and the loss of her mother's daily presence. Every morning she would cross a bridge going to school, which was located over the 220 West Highway. She would have suicidal ideas about jumping off this bridge and ending it all.

3

~~~

The destructive period eventually ended. Kanasia got tired of feeling sorry for herself, and she was ready to try to make things better in her life so she could escape this miserable living arrangement. Kanasia started getting involved in future career planning since she was already a junior in high school; before she knew it, she would be eighteen years old. She also became proactive and began speaking to the nurse at school to find out if there were any free programs for vision, health, or dental screening. Fortunately for her and her situation, there was, so she registered for these programs to take care of her health since the adults didn't care to.

Kanasia had a friend in her American history class named Maria. She was originally from South America and on the same route Kanasia walked to go to school. She lived in a house directly across from the 220 West Highway bridge Kanasia once entertained jumping off. They became close friends, and Kanasia met Maria's parents. She would often go to Maria's house along the way to school so they could walk together. Kanasia told Maria about her mother and situation at home with her brothers. Maria told her mother about Kanasia's situation, and her mother began to treat Kanasia as if she were her daughter. She cooked for Kanasia and wanted her to stay at their house when she didn't feel well. This friendship helped Kanasia make it through the rough times she encountered at home. It even made her feel more hopeful about life.

Kanasia began to apply to fast-food restaurants again just to get some cash in her pockets for transportation or to eat something she really wanted to eat. At school, it was time for yearbook pictures and class rings, and she wanted to obtain a job in order to get them. Kanasia wrote to her brother Rick to ask for his assistance with getting both. He came through and sent her the money every month until she finished paying for both.

She had no money to buy new clothes or even to get her hair done for her pictures. Kanasia was still wearing braided hair extensions from when she went to visit Paris during her break from school in February. But she had makeup, hair grease, and a good brush to make it work. The pictures turned out beautiful. She was so amazed, and for the first time, she began to see her beauty. In those pictures, there wasn't a line of misery, hardship, or depression displayed. Kanasia was so impressed when the proofs came. She chose the best two for the yearbook and gave out copies to family and friends.

Through the proofs, she realized that she was pretty enough to pursue a career as a flight attendant. Kanasia had always fantasized about traveling the world, and she figured working in this industry would be the best way to accomplish it. She didn't know how much longer her mother would be in the nursing home, but she knew she needed a good-paying job to make things turn around for them, even if it meant she couldn't see her mother every day.

At school, Kanasia found out about a recruiter for the Legions Schools for flight attendants, and she made arrangements to speak to the recruiter and find out about the requirements. One of the requirements was to have an interview with her family in their home in order to go over the program and see if Kanasia was a candidate for the flight attendant program. Kanasia knew she didn't want to do the interview at Eddie's apartment because he lived out of the school district, so she made arrangements to meet with the recruiter at Orain's house, which was near the school.

When she told Orain about her interest in attending a flight attendant school, he responded, "You aren't pretty enough for that job!"

Kanasia was so upset and didn't know why he was being so mean and negative to her. So she gave up on it and cancelled the interview with the recruiter. When the recruiter asked her why, Kanasia told her she was no longer interested.

It was now spring break. Kanasia spoke to her cousin Abel, and he planned for her to come down to Ohio. He even paid for her bus ticket. It was perfect timing because it was near her seventeenth birthday.

When Kanasia arrived, Abel and his sisters treated her so well. They took her clothes shopping, she went to church on Easter, and she even hung out with her younger cousins Valencia and LaCria. They went to the movies and talked about school and boys. They listened to music and watched television together. This was their first time meeting each other, and they clicked and had a good time.

But Kansaia was getting homesick for her mother and wanted to return, even though she had three more days to go. Kanasia called up the bus station to see when the earliest bus was. She called Abel and told him she was ready to return to Illinois. He was disappointed, but he understood.

He drove her to the bus station to return home. He had to drive like a bat out of hell because it was the last bus of the evening leaving for Illinois. She made it. Kanasia was so happy. She had had enough of that area and just wanted to come back home to familiar territory and her mom.

Kanasia arrived back in Illinois for her seventeenth birthday. She never received a birthday greeting, a cake, or a gift from Eddie, his family, or Orain. She was so heartbroken by this lack of acknowledgment, feeling as if she didn't exist.

Kanasia was ready to start dating now. She wanted to be loved and was ready to find that special guy. She continued to look for part-time work but was unsuccessful. Kanasia was so aggravated that she burned her working papers from school on the stove. She was so tired of trying and not getting anywhere.

It was almost time for school to be out for the summer, and she began to go to the nursing home every day. One day as she was sitting in her mother's room, her brother Randy and one of his friends from church, Kemell, came by to see their mother. Kemell was active in the military and was home on leave for a month. He started coming by the nursing home to see her mother every opportunity he could. During these days, Kemell would take her to get something to eat and give her a ride back to Eddie's apartment as well. Kanasia even brought him inside to meet Eddie, and there was never any resistance to his presence. Kemell was a handsome, polite, well-mannered young man living out his military dream.

Kemell was always respectful, a gentleman, and he always made sure Kanasia had something to eat and a ride home from the nursing home, and he even took her to a store and bought her a pair of pink shorts. She really wanted those shorts, and he didn't hesitate to buy them for her. But unfortunately, it was time for him to go back to his duties in the military. Kanasia was starting to become attached to him because she knew if no one else looked out for her, Kemell would.

4

Come summer, Kanasia began to go to the nursing home every moment she got. She didn't have anywhere else to go. She had no summer job and definitely no vacation plans. One day Kanasia came in early enough to go with her mother to her physical therapy session. This was a big surprise for Kanasia because she had never witnessed a physical therapy session before. The physical therapist came to pick up her mother from her room for treatment. The therapist's name was Angel, and she had a bubbly, cool, and friendly personality. Kanasia could tell she had a great rapport with her mother. They bonded instantly.

Angel referred Kanasia to an agency for summer employment as a transporter for the physical therapy department. She was hired right away. She worked for two nursing homes, transporting patients via wheelchair to their therapy sessions. Kanasia was so excited and happy that she finally had a summer job. She had to wear all white.

She gave the agency Orain's address for them to mail her paychecks. Kanasia was afraid that Eddie would take her checks. However, she was also afraid Orain would take her check, so she took the bus to his house on payday which was every other Friday, and she searched for her paycheck in his mailbox. Kanasia was successful, and her paychecks were there like clockwork. She opened a savings account at a local bank where she cashed her checks.

But in the midst of all this good news, Kanasia also had the opportunity to see her mother during her therapy session. She had no idea her mother could stand with assistance. She was so amazed and happy, and she cried tears of joy. Kanasia could remember the doctor saying that her mother would not be able to stand or walk again.

Week by week, Kanasia saw more improvement with her mother's physical therapy sessions. Angel was good with her and encouraged her to do more. Kanasia finally saw her mother walk again. She took a few steps with a quad cane in her right hand, and Angel was by her left side, where she had weakness and residual effects from the stroke. Angel also trailed behind them with a wheelchair in case her mother became tired or weak.

"What a blessing. Everything is starting to fall in place! Thank you, Jesus!" Kanasia said.

Angel was such a help to Kanasia and her mother. She became like family and was so easy to talk to. Every day began to look brighter and brighter for

Kanasia and her mother. She also saw a difference in her physically and mentally. She was motivated and working hard to get back to normal as possible. Even the feeding tube was disconnected, and her mother was eating regular food again.

Kanasia began familiarizing herself with the other staff at the nursing home, like the CNAs, nurses, social workers, and occupational therapists. She even familiarized herself with the woman that came in every month to give haircuts. Kanasia loved watching her get her hair done. Samantha's face would light up with so much joy and a big smile. She would talk up a storm and laugh with her. There was so much positive improvement and hope. Samantha was learning to adapt to her new life as a stroke survivor.

Kanasia was so excited that she asked Amy, the social worker, if she could assist them in finding an apartment nearby so Kanasia could take her mother out of that nursing home. Amy was an obese white woman in her forties who didn't take care of herself, came to work looking sloppy, and even enrolled in a fat camp to lose weight. She was a nice person, but she had some underlying issues with herself. She told Kanasia she would look into programs to help them. But unfortunately, she resigned and Kanasia and her mother were at a standstill.

Finally the nursing home found a replacement named Wanda. She was an attractive African American woman in her thirties. She had a heart of gold, overflowing with human compassion. She took to Samantha and Kanasia right away. Kanasia informed her that she wanted to get her mother out of the nursing home and that they wanted to move into an apartment in the area.

Wanda started doing her research to see if she could help them in obtaining an apartment. Wanda and Kanasia even went out to look for apartments together, but Kanasia didn't have enough money to cover the move or rent, which meant she had to keep her mother at the nursing home a little longer. This also meant she had to continue staying with Eddie.

But Kanasia didn't give up, and she kept working for the summer. Her mother was getting better with walking and was able to transfer herself from the bed to her wheelchair. Her mother's steps became stronger and longer. She could now walk a whole corridor with that quad cane. Meanwhile, Wanda continued looking for programs to assist them with paying their rent and contribute to the moving expenses.

Kanasia would be so exhausted after working that she would fall asleep in her mother's room. While she was sleeping in her mother's bedside chair, her mother would look at Kanasia and smile. The nursing home food was gross, so now that her mother was eating regular food again, Kanasia would bring her sausages, sardines, crackers, soda, cheese, lunchmeat, and some snacks. This way she wouldn't have to eat the food the nursing home served; it looked like mush for an animal and smelled like canned dog food.

The nursing home always had new staff, and Kanasia got to know every one of them. One day she noticed this little black guy with neatly ironed scrubs, white loud-sounding shoes, and curly long hair. He also wore so much damn cologne that between his shoes making *clickity, clackity* sounds and the strong aroma of his cologne, she knew when he was working. Kanasia would see him, but she would never speak, and sometimes he would stare at her too. This irked the hell out of Kanasia.

One day Kanasia repositioned her mother in the bed, but she pulled her up so fast and hard that she made a loud thumping sound. The little black guy with the loud shoes and strong cologne came running into the room. "Is everything okay in here? I heard a loud sound," he said.

Samantha was smiling, and Kanasia told him she just repositioned her mother in the bed.

"Be careful. Call if you need help!" he replied.

From then on, he started adjusting the television in her mother's room to clear the static and get a better picture. He introduced himself as Zilas. They began to talk, and he started checking on her mother every time he worked. He personally looked after her mother as if she were his own. Then one day Orain came when Zilas was working and came to find out they knew each other.

Kanasia said to herself, "What a small world!"

She began to wonder now if Zilas could be trusted since he knew Orain. But Zilas kind of grated on her nerves and Kanasia tried hard not to like him.

However, he was nice, had a sense of humor, and looked after her mother. She had no choice but to start liking and trusting him.

Zilas asked her out on a date. She was shocked because she knew he was at least in his late twenties to thirties. Kanasia was also suspicious of his sexuality. He was a little too neat, smelled too good, and had some feminine neatness with that hair. It was Jheri curled down and flowing. But on the flip side, he was so handsome with those hazel eyes, cool Caribbean dialect, and the long hair. He reminded her of the actor Tory Thomas from the soaps. Every time Kanasia came to see her mother, there was Zilas on the spot. He was being so persistent about going out on a date that Kanasia finally gave in.

But on the day of the date, she stood him up out of fear. Kanasia thought about him more and more each day. She realized that he was not a bad man, and if he took care of her mother like he did, then why not give him chance and go out with him?

So they had their first date, consisting of fried chicken and side dishes from a local restaurant, beer, and wine. Zilas took a large comforter from the trunk of his car, spread it out over the grass, and arranged the food so they could have a picnic by the lake. It was beautiful. No one had ever done this for Kanasia before. She had only seen picnic dates in the movies and on television. It was cool, and she liked it. They talked, laughed, and got to know each other more. He never got fresh or made any moves on her. He was a perfect gentleman, caring, taking an interest in her, and listening.

Kanasia was so happy she kept this date, and it helped her face her problems a little better because now she had someone—a man—she could trust and confide in. This was the beginning of a relationship between Zilas and Kanasia in which one date led to another. Their comfort level with each other was growing, and there was no separating the two of them.

They finally brought their relationship to the next level, and Zilas and Kanasia went back to his apartment. It was great making love to someone she really loved and who loved her back. It was like a brand-new world now, and every day was special because of him.

Zilas started taking Kanasia back to Eddie's house at night when she would leave the nursing home. But because of his age, she would never introduce him to Eddie or his family. One evening when Zilas dropped Kanasia off, Eddie's wife, Annie, was standing outside their apartment.

As Kanasia reached over to kiss Zilas goodnight, before she could get out of the car, Annie said, "I thought you were kissing a woman. Oh my God!"

She could be ignorant, disrespectful, and obnoxious at times. Kanasia ignored Annie and kept walking because she knew she had somebody that was going to look after her. The days of walking everywhere were over. Eddie and Annie l didn't even have a car.

Kanasia thought, *A new day has come!*

She lost all respect for Annie because she never intervened when Kanasia was being choked or screamed at by Eddie. She stood by and did nothing, and she would even come in the room where it was happening. Inside, Kanasia knew all of this bullshit was coming to an end.

5

One day Wanda approached Samantha and Kanasia about a program she was involved in with teenagers, which consisted of a sleepover camping trip to the mountains of Michigan for a weekend. Wanda asked Kanasia if she wanted to go and if her mother would give her permission to attend. Kanasia jumped at this opportunity because she'd never had a camp experience like her other siblings. This could be a nice quick getaway for her and give her a chance to relax, have fun, and meet new people too.

Kanasia told Eddie about the trip, and he gave his approval. She informed Zilas that she was going, and he too felt it would be a great experience for her. He would look after her mother while she was away.

That weekend came, and Wanda took Kanasia to the bus. Wanda was going too, but she drove up in her car. She didn't spend the nights up there because she had a boyfriend that she wanted to go back home to. Kanasia knew how she felt, especially now that she and Zilas were involved. Kanasia would miss Zilas so much, but they both knew she needed this trip.

There were about forty people on the trip, consisting of male and female teenagers as well as the camp counselors. The camp had row boating, kayaking, fishing, campfires, hiking, dancing, toga parties, and lots of food. Kanasia had so much fun at the camp by the lake. It relaxed her and calmed her spirit. She even bonded and exchanged telephone numbers with a few people that were there.

But it was now time to go back to Eddie's damn house. As Kanasia rode back on the bus to meet up with Wanda, she felt so frustrated again because of where she had to go back to after such a fun and peace-filled weekend. As Wanda and Kanasia approached Eddie's house, it was about two in the morning. Kanasia directed Wanda to pull up in the driveway by Eddie's apartment.

"Where are we going? Why are we going to the back of the building at this time of the night?" Wanda was looking confused and upset.

Kanasia explained to her that she had the key to the front door, but only to one of the two locks. The front door was always double-locked unless Eddie's family was outside or at the store. Kanasia said that every time she went out, she had to come in through the back of the apartment.

"This is not safe or appropriate for you!" Wanda said. "Anything could happen to you in this dark alley."

"I know," Kanasia told her, "but the front door is never unlocked, and this alley is my only access to the apartment."

Kanasia could see the curiosity in Wanda's eyes about her living situation with Eddie and his family. Wanda looked worried as well. Wanda gave Kanasia a hug, and Kanasia thanked Wanda for the camping trip. As Kanasia exited the car, Wanda watched her as she walked up the back stairs. She waited until Kanasia opened the back door before she drove off.

Kanasia went in the house. It was dark, quiet, and everyone was sleeping. She proceeded to her bedroom. At least she had some good memories to focus on and dream about.

It was Monday morning now and time to go back to her summer job. She would work and hang out with her mother at the nursing home. But her routine switched to hanging out with Zilas at night. They were inseparable, and Kanasia began spending more time at his apartment. She even stayed out a few nights in a row, and Eddie never even questioned it. However, Zilas did tell her that she should call Eddie and let him know she was going to be out so he wouldn't worry. So she did.

After interrogation from Eddie, he responded, "Have a good time!"

"Thank you, I will!" Kanasia said.

Kanasia knew she was going to have a good time with Zilas and they were in every way. Zilas was a reefer smoker, rum and Coke drinker, and occasionally took mescaline. It didn't take long for Kanasia to get into it too, and it made the lovemaking wild as hell. They took it to another level, and she enjoyed it.

She felt so relaxed until it was time to go back to Eddie's apartment. Kanasia dreaded that thought and wished she didn't have to go back. She didn't mind rebelling at this point because she finally had someone paying attention to her and loving her. She was experiencing sex, drugs, feeling free, and a man to share these encounters with.

But she was having too much fun, and she was happy that Eddie didn't like it. Trouble was about to begin. Even though Eddie wasn't voicing his concerns over her whereabouts, he and Orain were curious and cooking up some drama to find out who Kanasia was hanging out with.

One day Orain came to the nursing home, and Zilas was in their mother's room.

"Can I speak to you in the hallway?" Orain said to Zilas.

They left the room and had a conversation about Kanasia. Orain interrogated Zilas about their relationship and informed him that he could go to jail for statutory rape if he was involved with her. Zilas denied it and walked away.

At this point, the couple knew they needed to proceed with caution. If Zilas dropped Kanasia off, he had to let her out about two blocks from Eddie's apartment to avoid drama.

One night when Zilas dropped her off, he gave Kanasia a key to his apartment and his car. He told her that she never had to be on the street as long as he lived. "If you ever need somewhere to go or you need to wait for me in my car, you can," he said to her.

The atmosphere in Eddie's home was shifting from a moment of peace to calm before the damn tornado. No one in Eddie's family was communicating with her, food that Annie cooked was put away before she came home, and nasty dispositions were floating around all over the place. She now had to make sure she ate before she came home, because nothing was available to her. She had some money saved up, so she would sometimes go buy fresh fish for herself and her mother. She would take it back to Eddie's home, cook it, make mashed potatoes, and take it to her mother for their lunch.

Her nephew Michael was giving her mad attitude when he saw that she was using the stove to cook and that she bought her own food. Kanasia paid him no attention and kept doing what she was doing. He would walk around making stupid comments aloud about her cooking skills. Michael even called Annie to tattletale that Kanasia bought food and was using the stove to cook it. She ignored him, finished cooking, packaged up the food, and left for the nursing home.

Another weekend was coming up, but this time before she went out, Eddie approached Kanasia and told her she now had a curfew of nine every night, adding that she was not allowed to spend the night out anymore. She was a little upset, but she had to deal with it. It was hard, but Kanasia did it, and she made arrangements to meet up with Zilas on his days off.

Meanwhile, the verbal abuse from Eddie was starting up again. She did everything he asked, so she really didn't know what his problem was. Kanasia tried to stay positive and avoid any face-to-face confrontation with Eddie and his family.

One Thursday her sister came to town to see Kanasia and her mother. Paris flew into Illinois from Florida, and Kanasia met her at the nursing home. They didn't have a long time to spend with each other because she had a play audition in New York. Paris was leaving the same day she came, flying out at nine that night, and she asked Kanasia if she wanted to accompany her to the airport by taxi. Paris told her she would pay her bus fare back home. When Kanasia told her about her curfew at Eddie's, Paris said she would call him in advance to let him know she was with her.

Paris called and asked to speak to Eddie. She was on the phone with Annie. explaining to her she was in town and that Kanasia was going with her to the airport and might be a little late because of it. During the conversation, Annie refused to put Eddie on the telephone. She also let Paris know that regardless of her presence in town, Kanasia had a nine o'clock curfew. The conversation between Annie and Paris took a turn for the worse. The next thing Kanasia knew, Paris was going off on Annie, talking about the ill treatment she was receiving at their home. "You're an ignorant bitch," said Paris.

Kanasia was worried about getting home later that night and having to deal with Eddie.

Paris slammed the phone down on Annie, and they proceeded to the airport. Along the ride, they discussed the hostile environment that Kanasia encountered since living there and how it took place before her involvement with Zilas.

"It's like now that they know I have some type of support system, they're trying to break me back down and make me depressed again," Kanasia said.

Now at the airport, Kanasia hugged Paris and told her she would call her soon. Kanasia stayed in the cab and went back to Eddie's apartment. She was afraid to go back because she knew she would have to deal with the repercussion of Paris's conversation with Annie earlier that afternoon.

Although Kanasia arrived only about five minutes after her curfew, Eddie couldn't wait for her to get through the door before he approached her. Eddie was screaming and cursing at Kanasia about going over curfew.

"No one disrespects my wife, and you do not go over your curfew regardless of who's in town. I don't care!" Eddie screamed at the top of his lungs.

All Kanasia could do was listen. She would not dare to attempt to defend herself with him in this type of rage. She waited for him to calm down and walk away, but it took forever. It appeared that he had also been drinking, so the heat from his rage was more intense.

He began screaming, "I allow you to stay here. I should shoot you while you sleep for having disrespected my wife!"

Kanasia stood there trembling, and none of Eddie's children or wife came to see what the noise was or experienced the terroristic threats she encountered. She felt scared, nervous, and unaware of what was going to happen next. But she knew one thing: Kanasia had never had her life threatened before. When Eddie finally walked away from her, he was still cursing and yelling, accompanied by some nasty comments about Paris.

As he walked away, Kanasia started gathering her identification, clothes, makeup, and whatever else that would fit, cramming it all in her pillowcase. When the coast was clear, she ran down the front stairs and headed for the bus stop. She ran for her life. Kanasia felt as if she were doing hurdles to get down those stairs. It was as if she couldn't get to that street quickly enough. Her heart was racing with fear, and tears were now streaming down her face. Kanasia was so frightened that she kept looking to make sure Eddie wasn't following her.

She walked as far as she could up the street. Kanasia finally found a bus stop bench to rest, think, and contemplate what she was going to do or where she was going to go. She sat there with that pillowcase for a long time. All Kanasia could think about was why she had to go through these changes with Eddie and his family. If they didn't want her, then why did they take her in? She did

not deserve all this torture.

It was going on eleven o'clock, and she needed to decide what she was going

to do. Kanasia didn't want to involve Zilas, but didn't have anyone or anywhere

else to go. She decided to go to the nursing home to meet up with Zilas.

"If you ever need somewhere to go or you need to wait for me in my car,

you can," she remembered him saying. She decided to take him up on it tonight

because she did not want to sleep on the street, and he wouldn't want her to either.

Kanasia arrived at the nursing home at eleven twenty-five and went straight

to his car to wait for him. At midnight, Zilas clocked out of work and walked

toward his car in the parking lot. As he put the key in the car door, he jumped.

"Baby, what are you doing here? What happened tonight?" Zilas asked.

Kanasia explained to him everything that went down that night after

meeting up with Paris, as well as the torture she previously went through with

Eddie and his family. Zilas gave her a tight hug, and they drove back to his

apartment for the night.

Unfortunately, she had to work in the morning. It was getting late, and her

nerves were like a bundle of twine. Kanasia was so nervous that she was sweating,

and her heart was beating so fast that it felt like a drumbeat. She was crying

and couldn't relax or sleep, because of everything going on. However, it was fine

because Zilas cradled her in his arms all night long.

6

Zilas also worked at a small community hospital during the day, from six thirty in the morning until two thirty in the afternoon, Monday through Friday, as an orderly for the operating room. This was his full-time day job, and he had worked there for about fourteen years. When Zilas went to the hospital that morning, Kanasia stayed behind to try to sleep since she didn't have to be at work until eight at the nursing home. When she couldn't fall asleep, she started getting ready to leave for work.

While she was at work, Kanasia tried to forget what she went through with Eddie the night before. She threw herself into her work, but it didn't work.

"Kanasia, are you okay today? You're very quiet, and I've never seen you like this before," said Mark, one of her coworkers.

Kanasia just responded, "Yes, I'm okay."

She didn't know if she could trust him or if he would even understand her circumstances. He had his mother and father at home. Could he really understand or help her? She chose to keep it to herself until she met up with Angel and Wanda. Most of all, she did not want to get Zilas in any kind of trouble with the law or her crazy brothers.

When it was time for lunch, she and Angel went to get some fried chicken. Angel also picked up some Golden Champale for them to drink. They took the food back to the park to eat. As they approached the park, Kanasia asked Angel if she could confide in her about some problems she was encountering at home with Eddie and her current homelessness. As she began telling Angel about her situation, she saw her whole expression go from happy to shock. Kanasia could tell she felt bad for her, and Angel encouraged her to talk to Wanda to let her know what was going on.

Kanasia spoke to Wanda later that afternoon after she finished working for the day. She asked Wanda if she could find her somewhere to stay permanently, saying that she did not want to go back to Eddie's apartment. She feared for her life and felt that because she ran away, it was definitely going to get worse.

Kanasia was trying to avoid telling her mother of these ongoing problems, but Wanda told her she would have to let her know eventually because Kanasia may need her to get involved legally for authorizations. Samantha was still her legal guardian. All Orain did was make sure he collected Kanasia's social security checks every third of the month. He forgot about caring for her, feeding her, providing for her, and loving her.

Kanasia then informed her mother of what was going on at Eddie's house and about how Orain was not giving her food or bus fare money out of her social security check. When Wanda came up to her mother's room to speak to her about the situation, she told Samantha she would try her best to find Kanasia somewhere to stay.

"Where are you going to stay for the weekend?" Wanda asked Kanasia.

"I'll be staying at one of my classmate's house over the weekend," Kanasia said.

But her mother knew where she was really going to stay: at Zilas's apartment.

Wanda was about to exit her mother's room when she turned and said, "I'll find you a place so you do not have to return to Eddie's torture chamber."

Since Kanasia didn't sleep the night before, tiredness took her over as she sat in her mother's bedside chair. She was immediately sleeping, snoring, and drooling. When she did awaken, her mother was staring at her. Samantha watched over with a sad look in her eyes for the mistreatment Kanasia received at Eddie's and the disappointment of Orain's money snatching and deprivation efforts.

Kanasia stayed with her mother until the end of visiting hours, and then she took the bus to Zilas's apartment for the night. She was so nervous as she left the nursing home that she had to look all around before she opened the door to leave. She walked to the bus stop located two stops down from the nursing home just in case Orain or Eddie was waiting for her outside. The coast was clear, and she approached the stop as the bus was pulling up. As she got closer to Zilas's apartment she looked out the window to make sure she didn't see Eddie or Orain in sight. Those two had her so paranoid and nervous.

When Kanasia arrived at Zilas's, he prepared a hot meal for her, consisting of baked chicken, rice, and peas, accompanied with a rum and Coke.

"Good evening, honey," Zilas said as he reached over to hug and kiss her.

"Hi, honey. How are you?" she replied.

She was so glad to be back with Zilas, but she was nervous at the same time. She couldn't fully relax, because of her current circumstances.

As she and Zilas had dinner, they discussed her living situation to decide what Kanasia was going to do. She told Zilas that she'd spoken to the social worker at the nursing home and she was looking for her a place to stay. Zilas informed Kanasia that he did a little inquiring in the neighborhood about places for her to stay and receive her mail. He was friends with a few women in his apartment complex. He talked with them about Samantha being a patient in the nursing home where he worked and how Kanasia was still in high school but needed somewhere to stay until she graduated.

He told her that one of his neighbors named Ella told him that she could stay with her or use her address for her mail. Kanasia thanked Zilas because she did not want to involve him in her family problems or get him arrested. Their relationship was special, and she did not want to lose him. She needed Zilas more than ever. They continued their dinner and watched television afterward. Before she knew it, Sunday rolled around and it was time to get ready to go back to work the next day. Kanasia couldn't wait to see what arrangements or options she had with Wanda's research.

This was Kanasia's last work week at the nursing home due to it only being a summer job. She learned that she needed to give Wanda a few more days to do her research. Meanwhile, Kanasia was running out of clothes because all of them were at Eddie's place. Zilas gave her money to buy some outfits. She was so distraught that she wasn't initially worried about clothes, just her safety when she ran away.

Come Wednesday, Kanasia was still with Zilas. Wanda came up to Samantha's room at the end of her shift to let them know that she was having a difficult time finding Kanasia a place to stay.

When Samantha asked her why, Wanda replied, "Kanasia isn't on drugs or pregnant, and she doesn't have behavioral problems, so it's hard to place her. There are no programs for an honor roll student with good manners who needs a place to stay. For the programs that do exist, she would not fit in or they would cause more damage to her. She would not want to see Kanasia in any of these halfway houses or programs. She's a positive young lady that shouldn't be surrounded by negative adolescents.

"However," she continued, "there is one more option. I spoke to my family about Kanasia to ask if she could stay with us. But I would need you to put in writing that I have custody of Kanasia, and I would also need you to stop Orain from getting her social security check each month so she can support herself. In order to do, this I would have to take a letter from you to the social security office, giving me permission to receive Kanasia's check on her behalf until she is eighteen."

Wanda told Samantha that she and her family would charge Kanasia a monthly rent fee of eighty dollars for room and meals. Wanda asked them to think about it over the next couple of days and let her know. If Kanasia decided to go with this option, she could move in by the weekend. They told Wanda they would get back to her by Friday to let her know.

Kanasia and Samantha went over the details together. They both decided this was the best option for her to have somewhere to stay. It was also very nice of Wanda to make an offer like this and extend herself beyond the call of duty. They were so grateful to Wanda and her family for wanting to take Kanasia into their home. Kanasia called Wanda up to the room and told her that they decided to take her up on her offer. Wanda was happy and told her that she would be back to see them in a few minutes.

When Wanda returned, she had two letters typed up. One stated that Samantha gave Wanda guardianship over Kanasia until she was eighteen and in her care, and the second one was for the Social Security Administration, requesting a change in guardianship as well as a new mailing address for her check. Her mother signed both letters and gave them back to Wanda.

Kanasia contacted Zilas to let him know what she and her mother decided about her living arrangements. Zilas was relieved that she found somewhere to stay. He didn't want her in the wrong place and ending up with worse problems than what she had. She and Zilas agreed to meet up on the weekends and on his days off.

Kanasia and Wanda went to the local social security office on Monday to place the request. From that date on, Kanasia started living with Wanda and her family. She didn't have her own room but shared a room with Wanda. It felt awkward at first because she didn't know Wanda's family, but the atmosphere was much sweeter than Eddie's apartment. She could not complain at all, because they welcomed her with open arms and hearts.

Wanda's grandmother was so accommodating by making sure Kanasia always had something to eat. She wouldn't let her leave the house without eating. Grandma would say, "I gonna put some meat on those bones. You are so skinny!"

This was a new start for her last year of high school and great way to go into it. She had no worries about where she was going to stay or having to deal with abuse.

Kanasia's first social security check came to her address on September 3. It was about two weeks later that Orain discovered that she was no longer living with Eddie and his collection privileges of her social security check was over. It was a shame that neither Eddie nor Orain had looked for Kanasia or questioned her whereabouts until now. They showed no concern for her whatsoever. But once her check stopped going to Orain's house, he came up to the nursing home in a rage. He went into their mother's room screaming and yelling at her.

"You're too grown and out of control! What happened to your social security check? I haven't received it this month!"

"Calm down, Orain!" Samantha told him. "You are out of control, and it's not right how Kanasia didn't have food, bus fare, or money."

Kanasia became angry and screamed back at Orain, "You took my checks; I never saw a dime."

All of a sudden, Orain reached over and started hitting and scratching Kanasia's face. She was screaming and trying to fight back.

"Get off me!" she yelled.

Unexpectedly, her mother grabbed her quad cane and started striking Orain's back with it in order to get him off Kanasia. While her mother was beating his ass with the cane, Kanasia ran and called the police to report him.

The police came, as did the nurse in charge. They asked what was going on and why they did not alert the staff to this attack so they could deal with it.

"I didn't know what to do, and I was afraid," Kanasia replied. Her face was red, scratched, and bleeding above her left eyebrow.

The police asked the nurse if she had this under control, and they left. Orain grabbed his keys and headed for the door, stomping and clicking his heels as if he had on tap shoes. *Click, click, click.*

He didn't visit their mother for a few weeks after this incident, and when Kanasia saw him again, he had an attitude. He eventually started talking to them again. She knew he was more upset over the money than anything. Oh well. Kanasia didn't have any regrets for not being at Eddie's or disallowing Orain to receive her checks.

Wanda was good to her, and she gave Kanasia all of the money when the checks came. She took the rent money out of it, and Kanasia kept the rest for food, bus fare, clothes, and shoes, and she saved a little too. She also bought her mother food so she wouldn't have to eat the horrible food at the nursing home. Kanasia even bought her canned food for days she couldn't come to the nursing home.

7

It was a great feeling for Kanasia to get to the point of starting her senior year. She couldn't believe she would be graduating in nine months. Time had gone so fast, despite all the challenges she faced.

She was happy to have a place to stay, but she had a curfew at Wanda's, so she couldn't stay out with Zilas too late. It was so hard to go to him and not be able to spend the night. Kanasia was missing him so much. She was trying her best to stay focused on school and acclimate to her new home and family. Wanda wasn't that strict on Kanasia and gave her some flexibility. As long as she came back home before curfew and called her during the day to let her know she was okay, Wanda never harassed her about what she did on her days off.

Wanda was great, and she would later even take Kanasia to a few parties during the holidays. She said that Kanasia felt like her little sister and she was easy to talk to. Wanda even tried to help her get her driver's license by asking her neighbor if Kanasia could use her car for practice for the road test. She only wanted the best for Kanasia and tried in every way to keep her on point with school, transportation, and feeling comfortable with the new living arrangements.

Come October, Kanasia still had the remainder of her belongings at Eddie's. She told Wanda she wanted to go by and get them. Wanda was afraid for her to go alone over there, so they called Eddie to get permission to come by and pick up her belongings. No one answered the telephone, so they left a message on the answering machine, but the call was never returned.

Wanda decided that maybe it would be best to inform the police department of the situation between Eddie and Kanasia. She and Wanda went to the police department and explained everything. They also requested a police escort to Eddie's house in order to collect Kanasia's belongings. They did so when they knew he would be home from work. The police knocked on Eddie's apartment door and stated who they were. "It's the police. We're here for Mr. Eddie Jones on behalf of his sister, Kanasia."

Bang, bang, bang. Guess what. No answer.

They waited for about ten minutes before leaving. It was an unsuccessful trip, and Kanasia didn't know what she was going to do now. This man had the rest of her clothes, her stereo, her 8-tracks, and her makeup. Kanasia wanted to be done so she could move on with her future and never look back at that place, but this man wouldn't let her get her things. How mean and evil was that? She was out of his home, but he was still being vindictive and evil.

A few weeks passed, and Kanasia was trying to see how she was going to retrieve her things from Eddie without complications. Who could she use to intervene and help her? A little voice said, *Cousin Jose*. Kanasia listened to that little voice and called her cousin to request his help in getting her things from Eddie. Eddie and other family members respected Jose because he was one of their eldest cousins as well as her mother's favorite male cousin. Kanasia knew in her heart that she would finally get her things without any further hesitation.

Jose called Eddie in advance and arranged for her to come by to get her things. They went the next day in the evening. When Kanasia knocked on the door, Annie finally answered. She was cold and nasty.

"Your things are there!" she said, pointing to some garbage bags in the kitchen corner by the back door.

They had packed up all her things so she wouldn't have to walk around in their home. The stereo was underneath the four garbage bags with her clothes and 8-tracks. Eddie's house had a bad infestation of roaches and mice, so there was no telling what was crawling around inside those bags. They had packed her stuff up and thrown it in the kitchen as if she were a piece of shit. They had no respect for her or her things. But Kanasia was happy to get them and keep moving along. She never had to live in or look at that torture chamber again.

Jose and Kanasia drove away from Eddie's apartment and headed for Wanda's home. Her cousin lived about five minutes from Wanda, and she was finally able to introduce them. As she placed the key in the door, she noticed Wanda was leaving the house.

"Did you get your things from your brother?" she asked as she saw Kanasia's things on the porch.

Kanasia told her yes, with the help of her cousin Jose.

"Hallelujah. It's about time!" Wanda said.

"Yeah, I know. My clothes were being held hostage by Eddie."

Wanda was happy for Kanasia and thanked Jose for helping her out. She told him about how they went with the police and Eddie wouldn't open the door.

Wanda left the house, and Kanasia and her cousin took her bags upstairs to Wanda's room. As she opened the bags, roaches started running out of them. There were so many roaches that she had to leave the remainder of the bags in the basement and spray them down to kill any eggs or roaches hiding in them.

Grandma washed the clothes the next day, and she even folded them and placed them on the bed. Kanasia was so embarrassed about the roaches because Wanda's house was clean. She had never seen a roach in her two months at the house. Wanda understood because she saw the outside of Eddie's apartment.

It was approaching the fall holidays, and Kanasia wanted to spend time with Zilas. She and Zilas went out for dinner on his days off. One weekend Kanasia asked Wanda if she could spend the weekend at her friend Adri's house. Wanda didn't hesitate and said it was okay. Kanasia spoke to Adri to inform her that she used her name so she could spend the weekend with Zilas. Adri was okay with it, and Kanasia hung out with Zilas the whole weekend. Zilas surprised her by taking her to dinner, and they stayed in a motel.

Kanasia was already taking birth control pills, but she decided to see if the pills were working, so she skipped the Pill on the night they went to the motel. She was curious to see if she would get pregnant, because she had been taking the pills since she was fifteen. When Kanasia first started taking them, family planning told her to make sure she used a condom until her body adjusted to the pills to avoid the possibility of getting pregnant.

When Kanasia had sex for the first time, she was sixteen years old. It was with a guy named Clay. He was twenty-four years old, lived at home with his mother, and worked at the airport. They met one day while she was job hunting near Eddie's home, before she lived with him. Clay was amazed at her beauty, and they exchanged numbers right away. Whenever she was in town, she would call Clay.

One night they finally got together. Clay picked her up from Eddie's apartment, and they drove back to his house. They watched television, ate, and the next thing she knew, they were kissing. That led to the bedroom.

Clay was a fine, tall, slender guy with wavy long hair. He didn't offer much conversation, but he was nice. During this time, Kanasia wore wigs to give her an array of different looks. As they approached the bed, she wasn't about to mess up her wig, so she slid it off. They got busy, and she lost her virginity to Clay. He didn't use a condom either. He just jumped right on in. She never knew sex would hurt like that. She didn't find it enjoyable at all, and Kanasia felt as if she had gone horseback riding afterward. She couldn't walk well for a day or two, and she had to play this off by telling her mother she was sore from gym exercise at school.

Her period didn't come the next month. Kanasia was scared as hell and called Clay to let him know. He was scared, and he told her to keep him posted on it. Clay told Kanasia that if she needed money, to call him and he would pay for an abortion. She told him she would, but her period came a week later. Talk about being afraid and not listening to family planning staff about using condoms as a backup. Since she'd escaped this, Kanasia thought she might be sterile. She then skipped her pill with Zilas in order to see.

It was approaching Thanksgiving, and Kanasia started feeling nauseated, light-headed, and she began vomiting. Her breasts were fuller, her skin was glowing, her appetite had picked up, and she did not get her period. She told

Zilas that her period hadn't come yet. He told her to go take a pregnancy test as soon as possible. She made an appointment at the family planning clinic for the following week.

Kanasia sat in the examination room, cool and clammy from nervousness as she waited for the gynecologist to come in. When he finally came in the room, he asked, "What brings you in, young lady?"

"I haven't had my period yet. I'm about six weeks late. I'm on the Pill, but I've been nauseous and vomiting," Kanasia replied.

"Okay," the doctor said. "Let me examine you and we'll find out what's going on." As the doctor did his examination, his voice changed. "I know what's wrong. You're pregnant!"

"Oh my God. What am I going to do?" she replied. Kanasia sat there in disbelief, fear, nervousness, and disappointment.

The doctor gave her information about the possible options: having the baby, adoption, and abortion. He also told Kanasia that she needed to make a decision soon because the weeks were going fast. If she decided to terminate the pregnancy, she should do it as soon as possible to avoid complications or before the embryo was viable. He also gave Kanasia a list of clinics where she could have an abortion performed. She got dressed and left for Zilas's apartment.

He wasn't home from work yet, so she had time to decide how she was going to tell him. At three thirty that afternoon, Zilas pulled up in his driveway.

He immediately asked her, "How did it go at the doctor's?"

Kanasia couldn't prevent the tears from rolling down her face as she told him she was pregnant.

Zilas was quiet at first. "What do you want to do?" he finally asked.

Kanasia said, "I don't know. I can't believe I'm pregnant!" She started crying, and Zilas came to hug her.

"We'll work this out together. I'm here for you whatever you decide to do!" Zilas assured her.

Two weeks passed. Kanasia's nausea and vomiting episodes increased, but her skin was glowing, and it felt good to know that she was able to get pregnant. She was in la-la land, and she wasn't even thinking about terminating the pregnancy at first. Kanasia was also enjoying all the special attention from Zilas, but she knew she needed to make a decision soon because the weeks were flying by. She was now ten weeks pregnant. Kanasia thoroughly thought about the pregnancy and considered the advantages and disadvantages of having her baby.

She had to finish high school. There were only six more months until graduation, and she could hear Eddie's voice in her head saying, *You're going to end up pregnant!* In her heart, she could not give him, or the other family members, the satisfaction of watching her fail. Another thing she didn't want to do was have a big belly parading across the stage for her graduation. Kanasia decided to have an abortion, and she told Zilas what she decided to do. He understood, gave her his support, and she made the appointment to have the abortion the following week.

She never mentioned to anyone that she was pregnant except Zilas, and he accompanied her to the abortion clinic. They were both sad about the decision, but they knew it was for the best. She physically recovered from the abortion, but inside Kanasia felt disappointed, sad, and depressed with her decision. She swore to herself that if she ever got pregnant again, she would keep her baby without any hesitation.

8

It was now approaching Christmastime, and Zilas put up a tree and decorations. He even had gifts under the tree for Kanasia and her mother. She hadn't celebrated Christmas since before her mother took ill. It felt good, and there were many holiday parties going on at Wanda's house and Zilas's coworkers' houses. She and Zilas went to one of his coworker's New Year's Eve parties, and the food, drinks, and music were amazing. They had the time of their lives. They danced, laughed, and kissed. The night ended with a marriage proposal.

"I love you. Will you marry me?" Zilas said.

Kanasia was surprised. Tears streamed down her cheeks, and she was speechless. Then she looked into his beautiful hazel eyes.

"Yes," she replied. This was the best night of her life. She was drifting on a cloud. She never knew he wanted her in his life like that. Kanasia knew he loved her, but she was still surprised.

She couldn't wait to tell her mother when she saw her on New Year's Day. Kanasia told her that she and Zilas were going ring shopping but had not yet set a date. Samantha was happy for Kanasia and smiled with joy.

It was now 1983 and the weeks were going by fast. Kanasia was preparing for her graduation requirements, and she applied to the county college so she could take classes in September. She was unsure of her major at the time, but she applied anyway and was accepted. Truthfully, she felt like she needed a break from school; her heart really wasn't in it. All she could focus on was being Zilas's wife and being able to be with him without anyone's interruptions. She would soon be eighteen, and Zilas was about to turn thirty-five. Their birthdays were a week apart in April, and they planned to celebrate together. Kanasia couldn't wait, because she planned to move in with Zilas once she turned eighteen. She was anxious to tell Wanda she was moving out.

One day when Kanasia went to the nursing home to see her mother, Wanda came into the room and told them that the two qualified for a low-income apartment in Newark that was handicap equipped to make it easy for Samantha to move around. She told them all they had to do was fill out the paperwork and the apartment would be ready for them to move in at the end of the month. They were in disbelief. The day they had been waiting for was finally here. Kanasia's mother was getting out of the nursing home for good. Kanasia and Samantha were so excited and hugged Wanda.

Kanasia made arrangements with the storage company so they could deliver the furniture before she brought her mother home. She let Orain know, and he assisted with the move. The ambulance brought her mother to her new apartment, and as she entered the door, her eyes lit up with tears of joy.

Kanasia and her mother were living together again and adjusting to their new apartment. It was so good to be able to come home to her there and not the nursing home. In the beginning, it was just Orain and Kanasia who took care of their mom. Then the home health service was initiated. It was difficult for them at first because Kanasia couldn't leave her for long; she also had to come straight home from school to cook, make sure she was okay, bathe her, and help her up to the bathroom. Her mom was still a little unstable on her feet, and she needed that extra strength and set of hands to make sure she didn't fall.

It was now only three weeks away from Kanasia's high school graduation. She began to prepare for it by buying a dress, a pair of shoes, and planning her hairstyle. Zilas decided to pay for everything as an early gift.

Paris was back in town for the ceremony, and she stayed with them at the apartment. She planned the graduation party and sent out invitations.

It was graduation day, and Kanasia felt great accomplishment as she floated down the aisle while "Pomp and Circumstance" flowed through the arena. It was a bittersweet day because she knew she would never see some of her classmates again. But they had made it and were moving on with their lives.

The summer passed along, and Kanasia didn't have a job. She really couldn't have one due to her mother's health. It took a good two months before a nurse's aide was assigned to her, and once that happened, life became easier for them. It also allowed Kanasia more freedom to go out. She had missed Zilas so much, and most of her free time was spent with him at his apartment. Eventually, Paris moved in with her and their mother, and then about two months after that, Orain ended up moving in with them too. His four-year marriage with his wife was ending, and they were filing for a divorce.

When everyone moved into the apartment, Kanasia decided to move out. She felt it was time for some of her other siblings to help out with their mom, and she couldn't stand to be separated from Zilas any longer. She would still go back over to visit Samantha during the day to spend time with her, braid her hair, do her laundry, or cook if she needed her to. Because even though she wanted to be with Zilas, she still couldn't just walk away from her mom.

The summer was going by fast, and she was starting to feel hungry all the time. She would have cravings for lemons and limes, and she would suck on them as if they were grapes. She gained ten pounds, her skin was glowing, her cheeks were rosy, and her clothes fit tight like a glove. She blamed it on not being active and eating everything. But she didn't have her period for July or August, and then came the nausea and vomiting. She wasn't as worried about being pregnant this time around since she was an engaged adult who had graduated high school.

She went to get a professional opinion at the clinic and had to take a pregnancy test. This time she went in with anticipation that she was pregnant. The gynecologist came into the room and did her examination. As she completed the exam, she confirmed that Kanasia was indeed pregnant and would be due on March 14, 1984.

She was happy and couldn't wait to tell Zilas when he came home from work. Zilas had not purchased the engagement ring yet, and the two had not yet set a date for the wedding either. Kanasia didn't tell her mother or anyone else that she was pregnant. She wanted to keep the news to herself until she and Zilas decided to take more steps toward their futures together. She wanted to savor the thought of being able to keep her baby this time.

Even though Kanasia was spending time with her mother, Samantha was becoming jealous of Zilas. She knew he was the only thing keeping Kanasia away from her. Samantha began to talk about Zilas and Kanasia to her niece Marge on the telephone. One night Kanasia overheard her mother say, "Zilas ain't going to marry her!"

She was so upset that she had begun to cry. She couldn't believe her mother could say that, after Zilas had helped her when her own sons didn't. Once her mom was off the telephone, Kanasia approached her and asked why she had said that about Zilas.

"He's using you, and something is wrong with his blood!" she screamed at her. "Something's wrong with his blood!"

Kanasia ran out of the apartment in a rage, but she also felt disappointment and confusion. What did her mother mean, 'something is wrong with his blood'? Why was she trying to ruin her happiness with such vicious statements? She was so upset that she didn't even take the bus to Zilas's apartment. Instead, she walked for an hour to calm herself down. She felt that her mother was being mean or jealous in an attempt to break them up.

She had to take some time off from seeing Samantha after the outburst. Zilas attempted to convince her to go back over and talk with her mom, but she couldn't do it right away. She felt that she needed space from her mother, but that turned out to be the worst thing she could have done at that time.

All of a sudden, Eddie started to visit Samantha weekly. He had never visited their mother like that. Even when she was in the hospital or nursing home, he had only visited once or twice within a six-month period. These were not sincere visits. He was trying to take advantage of the situation. Due to their mother complaining about Kanasia and Zilas openly to their relatives, Eddie knew this was the right time to convince their mother to take out a life insurance policy on Kanasia. He also signed her up to get an American Express Credit Card.

Samantha was so happy that Eddie was spending time with her that she didn't see the bigger picture.

One day after Kanasia decided to go back and help her mother, she went to get some linens out of the bedside cedar chest to change Samantha's bed. In the chest, she saw a life insurance policy for fifty-thousand dollars for the insured that named two beneficiaries on it. The insured was Kanasia, and Samantha and Eddie were her beneficiaries. She was so hurt by this that she confronted her mom about it. She managed to convince her that Eddie was just using her to cause more conflict, and that he was also to trying to get money from her if she died. After the discussion, Samantha cancelled the life insurance policy as well as the credit card. When they cancelled the life insurance policy, Kanasia informed the company that her name had been forged. If they had refused to cancel, she told them she would sue for initiating the policy without her consent. She was so mad at Eddie.

Even though Samantha had fallen for his schemes, she and Kanasia made up. Her daughter started going over to see her again on a regular basis. Because of her mother's doubt about Zilas, the couple decided to keep their wedding and their pregnancy a secret until the time was right.

In September, Kanasia and Zilas decided it was time to get married. They went to city hall applied for their marriage license, had blood drawn, and did a counseling session at the Catholic Church around the corner from their apartment. They also went out to buy her engagement ring as well as their wedding bands. It was finally coming together. Kanasia went out to search for a wedding dress. She was able to find her dress, shoes, and a floral bouquet in the same area of town—all for a great price.

They set the wedding date for September 14, 1983 at two in the afternoon. At this point, Kanasia still hadn't told any of her relatives about the plans, but she did confide in her old high school friends Ariana and Ralaine. She asked Ariana to be the maid of honor, and she agreed. But as the time grew closer, Ariana stopped answering her calls. Kanasia started getting anxious about who she would choose as a replacement if Ariana would not come through. But God was good to Kanasia because she realized that she could ask Ralaine when Ariana fell through. Ralaine agreed enthusiastically.

As the date drew closer, Kanasia had gathered everything she needed and had gotten her hair styled the way she liked. The night before the wedding, she told Zilas that he had to stay with his brother and best man, Mark. That way Zilas couldn't see his bride before the ceremony. Kanasia was so happy, but she also afraid of making such a big commitment. She felt that her days of being a little girl were over now that she was about to become a wife and mother. She was also afraid, most of all, because she still hadn't told her mother. They decided to surprise her with the news after they took their vows since Samantha doubted them and couldn't keep anything to herself.

The sky was gray on the day of the wedding, filled with scattered cotton balls. It was cool outside, and there was a light rain drizzling down from the sky. The time seemed to be flying by so fast. It was soon time to get dressed and get to the church for the ceremony. As Kanasia approached the lobby of St. Leo's, Ralaine told her how beautiful she looked.

The service was held in the main sanctuary, which was lined with beautiful stained glass windows. There were candles lit everywhere, and the organist was in place nearby. Kanasia told her that she was nervous but ready nonetheless. As the two walked into the church, Zilas, Mark, and his girlfriend walked in the side door of the chapel. They were all there now, and they waited for Father Sonata to come to the front of the alter to perform the ceremony.

Father Sonata approached Kanasia and asked, "Are you ready, my dear?"

Then he began to lead her to the lobby of the church, where she would make her entrance into the sanctuary to begin her walk down the aisle.

"Yes, I'm ready," she replied, feeling a burst of joy and fear.

Ralaine walked in front of her down the aisle as the organist began to play a harmonious melody. It was beautiful. As Kanasia approached the sanctuary, "Here Comes the Bride" rang out and echoed through the air, sounding crisp. It made her feel so proud and beautiful. As she slowly approached the alter, she saw Zilas standing there. He looked handsome and nervous too. They both looked sharp and beautiful. While the ceremony was small, it was elegant. All eyes were on them as they stood side by side and proclaimed their vows before God. Then the organist played and sang "Ave Maria." It was so special, beautiful, and memorable. The only thing missing was her mom, but they had done what they had to do to make it happen. They were now Mr. and Mrs. Zilas Drummond. They had started a new chapter in their lives as a married couple.

Kanasia's belly was growing quickly, getting rounder and rounder. Her morning sickness was also increasing in frequency day by day. Her appetite was nonexistent because of the constant nausea. The morning sickness turned into all-day-and-night sickness. She felt so bad that she put her pillow on the floor in the bathroom and made it into her bed since that's where she always ended up. She was due for another physical with the obstetrician, and she hoped that he could recommend something to combat the morning sickness. The doctor placed her on a prenatal vitamin, vitamin B6, and a diet of crackers, soups, and ginger ale. He also scheduled her to come in every month for checkups and ultrasounds.

Kanasia and Zilas decided it was finally time to tell her mother the good news they had been withholding from her, that they had gotten married two months ago. They went over one afternoon and sat down to speak to Samantha. They wore their wedding bands and were smiling from cheek to cheek. Her mother didn't notice the rings right away, but Kanasia brought hers to her attention by placing her hand on Samantha's.

"We have some good news and a surprise for you!" Kanasia started.

"What, Kanasia? What is it?" she replied with excitement.

"Zilas and I got married in September, and I am expecting your grandbaby in March!"

Her mother was shocked. Her eyes widened, but her face gleamed with joy. "Congratulations to both of you! I'm so happy, and you're pregnant too!"

They had a group hug, and her mother couldn't wait to tell the rest of the family and her friends. She started making calls before they had even left. Samantha knew she had the gift of gab when it came to gossiping. Kanasia was glad that the secret was out, though, and she was looking forward to being able to relax and really start enjoying her life.

By the sixth month of her pregnancy, the nausea and vomiting began to decrease. She was finally able to eat again and tolerate different foods. She enjoyed reading books and magazines about what to expect in her pregnancy and her baby after its birth. She was fascinated but scared about all the changes that were going on. Then there was the thought that she had a little girl or boy getting nourished and growing inside of her. She started to feel a fluttering sensation in her belly that was occasionally accompanied with ripples of movement. She felt her first fetal kick and had to grab Zilas's hand to place over her belly. They were so excited about the baby's movements once they could be felt and seen on the exterior of her belly. She felt as if she had a little astronaut inside her. She started talking and singing to the little one inside of her daily.

She loved the special attention that Zilas, her family, and her friends gave her. She began to pick out potential names; she bought a few pairs of baby clothes and some bottles. Zilas was old-fashioned and believed that buying baby items in advance would give them bad luck, so Kanasia hid them in one of the closets to avoid hearing him protest.

The holidays were approaching, and it was their first Thanksgiving together as a married couple. Unfortunately, though, Zilas had to work. But Kanasia fixed her first Thanksgiving dinner and invited her mom, Orain, and Rick. It was tasty for her first Thanksgiving dinner. She cooked a turkey, a ham, some collard greens, candied yams, rice, string beans, and sweet potato pies. They all ate and enjoyed themselves, and she saved a plate for Zilas. It was a great feeling to have family around, to feel loved, and to have a wonderful, supportive husband. It was great to be in her own place, living life in splendor.

The months went by quickly, and that due date was getting closer. The closer it got, the more fearful Kanasia became. She wanted to take Lamaze classes, but Zilas was working two jobs at the time, and she didn't have anyone else to be her partner. As such, she was unable to take the classes, but she reached back into her new parenting magazines and found out about some exercises and breathing techniques to make the delivery easier. She wanted to prepare herself as much as possible. Kanasia and Zilas also took a tour of the hospital's labor and delivery rooms. This was helpful too, and it gave Kanasia some relief. She knew what to expect and where the birth of her child would occur.

It was now March of 1984, and the nausea and vomiting started again. Kanasia wondered if it was going to be an early or late delivery. She stayed closer to home and stopped taking the bus to be on the safe side. She also kept a bag packed by the front door in case she had to go to the hospital.

On Wednesday, March 7, Kanasia had a good day without morning sickness, and she slept until about twelve thirty in the afternoon. She was about to eat something and watch the soap opera *All My Children* on television when she suddenly felt a cramp in her belly. As she stood up to go to the bathroom, there was a gush of water on the floor by her feet.

Oh my God, is it time? she wondered.

Kanasia called Zilas at work right away to let him know what just happened. She could hear the nervousness in his voice.

"Call the doctor," he told her, "and I'll be on my way home to you."

Before she could hang up, she felt another sharp pain, one after another. The pains were coming about every three to five minutes apart, but more powerful each time. Kanasia called the doctor, and she was told to go directly to the emergency room because she was in active labor.

Zilas's friend Carlos was at home, and since he lived only five minutes away, he took her to the hospital instead. She could tell Carlos was nervous too, but he had two children of his own, and he knew the routine. When they arrived at the emergency room, the hospital staff was waiting for Kanasia with a wheelchair to take her directly to the labor and delivery unit.

As she was wheeled up to the unit, the nurses began to prepare her for delivery.

Kanasia was in so much pain, and she could not endure it any longer, so they gave her an epidural for the pain.

"When is the doctor coming?" she asked.

"He's on his way. You'll be having the baby in the next hour or two," the nurse replied.

Kanasia was so scared, but Zilas held her hand and comforted her once he arrived. The nurses guided her when it was time to start pushing.

Kanasia was glad to see Dr. Roma arrive. He told her to start pushing. As she was pushing, the staff began to move her into the delivery room. The head was slowly coming through, and Dr. Roma guided the rest of the baby's body out of the birthing canal. Then the final push.

"It's a girl!"

Kanasia was so happy. The screams of an infant filled the air. Shannon Valencia Drummond made her entrance into the world on Wednesday, March

7, 1984, at 4:46 p.m. She weighed seven pounds and nine ounces. She was beautiful, healthy, and strong.

Kanasia and Zilas were now proud parents and happy as can be. Family and friends came over to see little Shannon. She was a good baby, slept well, and didn't cry a lot. Kanasia cuddled her, sang to her, played all types of music for her, and read to her on a daily basis. She showed her and dressed Shannon in dresses and little ruffled socks at every possible opportunity.

Kanasia would take Shannon to her mother's place and her friends' houses. They prepared her christening at the same church where they were wed. Since Carlos was the person that took her to the hospital, they made him Shannon's godfather.

Shannon was growing so fast, and Kanasia and Zilas decided it was time for her to have her own room. They relocated to a larger apartment with two bedrooms in Bloomfield, which was about ten minutes away from Zilas's job. When Shannon was six months old, Kanasia began working as a dietary menu clerk as well as an aide in a community hospital.

Zilas purchased Kanasia's first car so she could get around and avoid having to carpool. It was a 1980 Mercury Capri, similar to a Ford Mustang but with a hatchback feature.

Kanasia was so happy, and things were moving along. Zilas had always wanted to purchase a home, so they worked hard and diligently for the next two years to save up for a down payment on a house. They started house hunting to get their motivation rolling.

At the end of spring in 1986, Kanasia told Zilas she wanted another baby so Shannon could have a little brother or sister to play with. They had also planned for them to be at least three years apart.

In August, she went to her gynecologist for a routine checkup. "Congratulations!" he told her. "You are pregnant and due on the nineteenth of April, next spring."

Kanasia was not surprised, and she had been waiting to hear this good news. She and Zilas were hoping this baby would be a boy and an Aries since they were both Aries. She couldn't wait to tell Zilas the good news. This also led them to look for a house on a daily basis.

With this pregnancy, Kanasia had very little morning sickness, and she was able to continue working up until her seventh month. Little Shannon was now two and a half years old and in the process of potty training, and Kanasia was preparing her for the arrival of a new baby brother or sister.

They continued to search for houses, and in October of 1986, they found a two-level single-family house in Lawrenceville, Illinois. It came with awnings and an enclosed sunporch. There were three spacious bedrooms, a furnished attic, a nice size backyard, and an unfurnished basement. It was a lovely colonial built in 1912 on a main street. It was missing a fireplace, garage, and driveway. But the hardwood floors, large rooms, and wood moldings were outstanding.

Zilas fell in love with this house, so he and Kanasia placed a contract on it with the realtor. Since they were first-time homebuyers, the down payment was only one thousand dollars. The buyer accepted their contract, and they proceeded to purchase the home. They were so happy with this decision that they would drive by the house to look at it every opportunity they got.

Their house closed on March 17, 1987. Kanasia and Zilas felt so good about accomplishing this goal together. They could have a bedroom for each child and a backyard for them to play in and barbecue.

They were so excited and full of plans for each room. As the weeks went on, Kanasia organized each room as her delivery date got closer and closer. She could not wait to have the baby and began planning the color scheme for the nursery. Zilas put the crib together while she decorated the room. Kanasia and Shannon would have bedtime stories every night, accompanied by the Lord's Prayer. During the day, Kanasia would take her out in the backyard to play, and they would order Domino's Pizza for lunch.

April was finally here. Kanasia felt anxious to have this baby and hoped it would be early like Shannon was. Her sleep pattern changed and she became an insomniac, so she got most of her sleep during the day. Shannon went along with the program and took naps during the day along with Kanasia.

April 19 was here and no labor. "Oh no," Kanasia said, "where is the baby?"

She was ready mentally and had a bag packed by the front door for her and Shannon. They made arrangements for Shannon to go to her mother's apartment with her and Paris when Kanasia did go into labor. All of their plans were in place, but she wasn't in labor yet. Kanasia was disappointed, but she gave up on that due date and started focusing on cleaning and continuing to plan the decor for the rest of the house.

Lo and behold, on Tuesday, April 28, 1987, Kanasia was finally in labor.

"Halleluah!" she exclaimed. She was praying for another four-hour labor. Zilas picked her up with a look of nervousness in his hazel eyes. He was moving quickly. They dropped Shannon off with Paris, and they were on their way to the hospital for delivery. The contractions were stronger and more consistent in timing.

When they arrived, a nurse was waiting for them with a wheelchair. The nurses quickly prepared Kanasia for delivery, and the doctor was already there. As the nurses began to connect her to the fetal monitors, one told her, "You will be delivering your baby in the next hour. Also, it's a girl!"

"How do you know?" Kanasia asked them.

"We can tell by the heartbeat. A female's heartbeat is much faster," the nurse replied.

"Well, Christopher is now Charlotte Michelle Drummond," Kanasia said.

At 5:43 p.m., Charlotte was born. They were filled with joy. She had another beautiful baby girl at seven pounds and five ounces. They decided to nickname her KiKi.

Kanasia and Zilas were so excited to bring home their new baby. It felt like another new beginning and a prosperous year for their family. Zilas immediately went back to work to support his family. He was such a good husband, father, son-in-law, friend, and provider.

Kanasia adjusted to caring for two children and the house. It wasn't too bad, because Shannon was a good child and very cooperative. She enjoyed having a little sister to play with and help with. Kanasia still felt a little sore from the delivery of Charlotte, but she managed to get back into her routine at home by doing the laundry, cooking, and keeping the house clean. The big challenge for her was the size of the house, along with all the stairs. This required her to be on her feet a lot, as she had to keep running up and down the stairs. Kanasia's weight dropped very fast because she didn't have any assistance from her family members.

During the month of May, Zilas began to complain about feeling tired and having a loss of appetite, and he also lost weight. They both blamed his symptoms on his working too much with the two full-time jobs and not getting enough rest. Zilas began to look sick, pale, and weak.

Kanasia encouraged him to make a doctor's appointment to find out what was going on with his health. He scheduled a doctor's appointment the following week. When he went in, the doctor conducted some lab tests. The doctor felt Zilas had a virus, so he placed him on antiviral medication. Zilas began to feel better.

As the Fourth of July approached, Kanasia and Zilas decided to have their first official barbecue. It turned out to be a blazing hot day, and no clouds were darkening the skies. They had about ten family members and friends over.

Kanasia picked up her mother, and they drove to pick up her friend Carmen. When they approached Carmen's apartment, she said she'd decided not to go, so Samantha and Kanasia drove back to the house alone.

They walked toward the backyard with sweat running down their faces because of the sun beaming down on them. Kanasia grabbed a chair for her mother and quickly assisted her to the chair. She gave her a cold glass of water to quench her thirst.

Before Kanasia could go inside to bring Zilas the ribs and chicken for the grill, Samantha began to complain of not feeling well.

"I need to go lie down inside. It's too hot out here!" she said.

Kanasia and Zilas ran over to her to help her inside and lay her down in their bedroom. Orain moved out of their mother's apartment the 3rd week in June, then Paris moved out a few days before the 4 th of July barbeque.

so their mother was now living alone. At this point, they decided that they were not going to allow Samantha to live alone another day. Kanasia and Zilas approached her mother and told her she was moving in with them. Samantha didn't object to this decision but instead welcomed it with a smile.

The following day, Zilas and some of his friends rented a truck and moved all of Samantha's furniture into their home. The Tuesday after the Fourth of July holiday, Kanasia called her mother's home health agency to inform them that she moved and that a nurse's aide was needed at her new location. They informed her that services would resume. They were now all under one roof. The worry of something bad happening to her mother while being at home alone was over.

Come July, Kanasia was ready to work again, so she began to apply for jobs. She took the girls to a babysitter for a few hours while she searched for jobs. She went to the hospital where Zilas worked and placed an application for several different departments.

Before the week ended, she was called in for an interview for their new department called Transport Services. Kanasia was hired as the manager and acting dispatcher of sixteen employees that provided labs and patient transport services throughout the hospital. She accepted the position and began working in August, so the children were off to a babysitter.

Kanasia was glad to be able to make her own money again and contribute to paying the bills so Zilas wouldn't have to work so hard. She would miss being at home with the girls, but she could not be a stay-at-home wife and mother. She also loved her job; she enjoyed delegating and all the perks of being in charge.

But along with this territory came jealousy from other workers in various departments at the hospital. They questioned why she was the one hired for this position and why they hired someone who was only twenty-one years old. Kanasia had to stay on her toes and ignore the negative gossip and hateful comments circulating throughout the hospital.

At the same time, she enjoyed being the in charge. Every day was like a fashion show when she appeared at work wearing her sophisticated, stylish, and sexy business attire, accompanied by her walk of confidence and hue of pride. She knew she had an audience, so she gave them a good show and maintained the department with a strong managerial structure.

11

When October came, Zilas started to feel sick again, but his symptoms grew worse than before and spiraled in a different direction. His skin began to look mottled, with tints of purple to gray tones, and he had sunken eyes and cheekbones. His clothes began to fit as if they were hanging off a clothesline by clothespins. Every night the pillows and sheets would be soiled, drenched in perspiration. He would also continuously sleep. It was not like Zilas to stay at home in bed sleeping, let alone calling in sick several days in a row.

Kanasia was overcome with worry and fear. Her nerves were causing her to jump at every little sound, along with a loss of appetite and sleepless nights. Zilas went to work after a few days. He tried to push forward and not give in to the sick feeling he was experiencing. But Kanasia knew he still didn't feel or look good. She had to get stern and convey to him that he needed to go back to the doctor so they could find out what was going on. He convinced her that he would make an appointment, and then he went straight to the bedroom to lie down.

Kanasia and Zilas went to the doctor the following day, and the doctor prescribed Zilas an antibiotic this time. He gave him an order to have a chest X-ray too. They had the prescription filled at the pharmacy.

When they arrived home, Zilas attempted to eat some soup, but he was unable to hold it down. He took the antibiotic and went to bed. Kanasia went upstairs to check on him, and she noticed that he was very restless. After a few hours, he drifted off to sleep, and she curled up next to him, cradling him in her bosom.

As the night grew, he developed a gurgling cough. He began to complain of chest discomfort, shortness of breath, and chills. His complexion grew pale, with his skin radiating heat. Zilas's restlessness increased, and his alertness was now blurred with clouds of confusion.

"Honey, it's time to go to the emergency room. No more delays. This could be pneumonia!" Kanasia stressed.

She put him and the girls in the car and drove him directly to the hospital emergency room. Along the ride, he was hallucinating and sweating profusely. Kanasia placed her foot firmly to the gas pedal, soaring with speed up the highway to the emergency room entrance.

The nursing staff took him to the back to be examined. He was placed on oxygen and his vital signs were taken and lab work done. They also took a chest X-ray. Kanasia and the girls stayed at his side, waiting for the test results. He was in so much pain, and he began to cry.

"Honey, don't cry! We're going to find out what's going on!" Kanasia said. "I love you, and we're here for you!" She reached over to hug and console him as a flow of tears escaped their eyes and flowed down their cheeks.

"Honey, I love you," Zilas said in a sad voice.

The doctor came in and informed them that the development of pneumonia was the reason for Zilas's symptoms.

"We need to keep you in the hospital, Mr. Drummond, for a few days so we can run more tests," the doctor said.

Kanasia felt helpless, frightened, and depressed, and she hated to leave him in the hospital. But she knew this was the best place for him to get the proper tests performed and discover the reason for his discomfort.

It took about four hours until Zilas was placed in a room on the second floor of the hospital. Once he was moved and comfortable, Kanasia and the girls left for home. She told Zilas that she would come back up to the hospital the next day before picking up the kids from the babysitter. They arrived home, and Kanasia put the girls in bed for the night.

She then went into her mother's room and sat on her bed weeping. She told Samantha about Zilas being diagnosed with pneumonia. They stayed up for a few hours talking and praying, with Samantha offering Kanasia words of encouragement.

She was so distraught that she couldn't eat, sleep, or focus on work, which she had no desire to go to. But Zilas was hospitalized, so she needed to keep the money coming in to support their household. The atmosphere in the house felt like an empty tin can that was deserted and thrown on the ground, left to roll aimlessly out of control.

The next day, the doctors planned various tests for Zilas. He was also placed on another floor in the hospital. The room had a large exterior windows and an entrance area with a sink. However, the door to his room was closed. Outside the room was a cart with yellow gowns, face masks, and gloves. A big sign on the doorframe of the entrance to the room stated isolation. This was new for Kanasia, and she didn't quite understand the meaning of it. She wondered why Zilas needed to be isolated from the other patients. Kanasia went up to the nurse's station for an explanation.

"Hello. I'm Zilas Drummond's wife, and I would like to speak to his nurse and doctor to get an update on his condition," she said.

Zilas's nurse came forward to the desk and introduced herself as Florence. She began to inform Kanasia of the tests that were conducted and explained to her that the reason for his being in an isolation room was to prevent any possible spread of infection.

"I'll page the doctor for you so you and your husband can discuss the test results and the other tests that have been ordered," Florence replied.

Kanasia noticed that Zilas wasn't feeling any better and his breathing was worse than before, along with the discoloration of his skin.

"Good afternoon, Mr. Drummond. Who is this pretty lady here with you?" Dr. Montez asked.

"This is my wife, Kanasia," Zilas replied, smiling.

"It's a pleasure to meet you, and I understand you'd like to discuss your husband's condition," Dr. Montez responded. "We're not quite sure what else is going on besides the pneumonia, and there is a possibility that he might have a collapsed lung. We're going to continue to conduct tests and also do a lung test, called a bronchoscopy, to determine his breathing problem."

"Okay. Well, thank you, Dr. Montez. Please keep me posted on his condition," Kanasia said.

Dr. Montez nodded as he exited the room.

Zilas was talking and in good spirits, despite his symptoms. Kanasia tried not to look upset, frightened, or cry in front of Zilas. Deep down, she was scared as hell, and she didn't know who she could talk to about Zilas besides his brother and her mother.

Kanasia continued to go to work, but her concentration was not there. It was going on a week since Zilas entered the hospital, and they had no answers yet about his condition. As she was trying her best to work, all of a sudden rumors began to circulate throughout the hospital that Zilas had AIDS. Kanasia was upset that someone could be so cruel and heartless to start this type of rumor. She tried her best to ignore the rumor because they already had many enemies due to her managerial position. People were jealous of them as a couple and the purchase of their home. She never gave it much thought and just interpreted it as a bad prank someone was playing on them.

As the work week grew, the rumors became stronger. They developed into such a serious problem that employees in the hospital started coming to her department and confronting Kanasia about the rumors. In particular, a tall African American woman who worked in the business office at the hospital came barging into her office. She introduced herself as Ruth, and she informed Kanasia that her children used the same babysitter.

Then she was screaming at her. "Does your husband from the OR department have AIDS?"

Kanasia just stood there, shocked that she would approach her like this. Her emotions changed to rage, and she became furious with her.

"Stop your accusations! How dare you barge into my office like this!" she yelled back.

Kanasia explained to her that Zilas had pneumonia and the possibility of a collapsed lung, not AIDS.

The woman didn't believe her and insisted that Kanasia tell her the truth. At this point, Kanasia asked her to leave, but she refused.

"Leave my office now, and if you return, I'm going to kick your fucking ass!" Kanasia replied.

"You're putting my children at risk for contracting the disease by bringing your children to the same babysitter!" Ruth screamed. "And by the way, I called the babysitter to let her know about these AIDS rumors, so be prepared for a telephone call from her."

As the woman stood in the office doorway, Kanasia ran to the other side of the room and pulled an intravenous pole from a wheelchair. She had started going toward Ruth to hit her when one of her workers walked in.

"What's going on in here?" Chris asked.

The room was now filled with a cloud of silence and a drift of tension in the air. Ruth decided to leave, but not without a threat. While she was walking away, she turned toward Kanasia and said, "I'm going to call the hospital where your husband is and find out his diagnosis!"

"Go ahead and try it and I will sue you and whoever else is involved in this with you," Kanasia replied.

After Ruth left, Kanasia sat down to regain her composure. However, Jane, the babysitter, called her to inquire whether the rumor was true. Kanasia tried her best to explain Zilas's condition in a calm tone, but she could hear in Jane's voice that she refused to accept what Kanasia was telling her.

"If this rumor is true, then that means that your daughters and the kids I babysit will all have to be tested for AIDS," Jane began telling her. "I don't feel comfortable watching your kids or even changing their diapers under these circumstances. Please come get them now!"

Kanasia couldn't believe her ears, whether this was actually happening. Kanasia knew Jane wanted her to pick up her children as soon as possible, so she told her, "I'm on my way!"

Kanasia hung up the telephone and went into her supervisor's office to inform him that she had an emergency with her children's babysitter and needed to pick them up.

Kanasia was hurt, humiliated, and angry, and she began to cry as she approached the bathroom. She couldn't erase the pain she felt, and the tears flowed continuously.

She finally calmed down after about fifteen minutes, and she left work to go get her children from Jane's house. However, Kanasia was still upset, and it began to affect her driving. She almost hit two cars and a pedestrian. Her concentration was off, and her emotions were soaring with rage. She felt as if someone had just thrown a grenade at her head and blown up her life, destroying everything their family had. She wondered who could be so cruel and cold. She hadn't done anything to deserve to have her and her family treated this way.

Kanasia arrived at Jane's to pick up the children. Jane didn't even speak; she just brought them to the door with their belongings and swiftly slammed the door. The tears began to flow from Kanasia's eyes as she walked to her car and returned home for the night.

She explained to her mother what had happened and that she no longer had a babysitter to watch the girls.

"I feel like I'm in a bad nightmare! What am I going to do now?" Kanasia asked.

The following day, Kanasia was unable to go to work because she had no babysitter. She tried to find someone to watch the children. She didn't want to tell Zilas about what happened with the job and the babysitter, but she had no choice since rumors were continuing to flow. She didn't want Zilas to worry about anything but his health. However, the rumors reached him at the hospital when one of his coworkers came to see him.

Since Kanasia was unable to attend work for a few days, she spoke to her assistant, Mary, to inform her of the problems she was having at work with the rumors and the problem with the babysitter. Talking to Mary was the worst thing she could have done. Mary made the situation worse by informing the other staff in their department that Kanasia had called her about the rumors.

Mary encouraged the staff to use every precaution they could when working with her to avoid contracting AIDS.

Because Kanasia still didn't have a replacement babysitter, she was forced to leave three-and-a-half-year-old Shannon and seven-month-old KiKi with her mother so she could go back to work. Samantha only had the use of her right arm and hand to grasp things due to the stroke. But with the help of Shannon, her mother made out okay with changing KiKi's diapers and feeding her.

12

When Kanasia went back to work, she noticed that the members of the staff were carrying around alcohol pads and wiping the telephone and desk down every time they used them. Every time one of her employees sat at her desk to answer the telephone, he or she would wipe all the surface areas down with alcohol, and they even started spraying the office with Lysol. They didn't care if Kanasia saw them or not.

The only one that didn't do this was Chris. She could tell that Chris felt sorry for her experiencing all this drama. One day when no one else was in the office, Chris came to Kanasia and hugged her.

"It's going to be okay, Mrs. Drummond. Don't worry about those crazy idiots," he said. Kanasia felt better knowing not everybody was after her.

As the days moved forward, Kanasia's head was swirling with all kinds of emotions, ranging from love, confusion, discomfort, depression, hopelessness, frustration, pain, fear, agony to hatred.

The weekend was approaching and her babysitter search was on. Kanasia began to inquire through some of Zilas's friends, and she found out that the wife of his friend Jermaine was not working. So Kanasia called her up and asked her if she could come by to discuss a babysitting proposition with her. Her name was Nancy, and she and Jermaine had seven children.

Nancy was a stay-at-home mother, and when Kanasia asked her about watching Shannon and KiKi, she was excited. She was even more willing when Kanasia told her that she would pay her weekly and provide her with transportation to do her own food shopping. This worked out great, and Nancy wasn't far from her job, so it allowed Kanasia to go back to work without the worry of having to find a babysitter.

Going on three weeks since his admittance, Zilas was still in the hospital. There were still no answers to all these tests. Kanasia's worries were escalating, along with her blood pressure and anxiety level.

It was another week and back to the routine of dropping the girls off at the babysitter and then off to work. Kanasia felt so alone and deserted at work, and she didn't know who she could trust anymore. As soon as she conquered the babysitter challenge, another one turned up. Chris told Kanasia about a petition that was going around the hospital to have her fired from her job.

Kanasia's staff and other employees in the hospital were requesting signatures to have her removed from her job as manager of the department because of the AIDS rumors. There was also a policy in place stating that relatives could not be employed at the same hospital, regardless of the departments. Once the petition was taken to the human resource department, she was informed by Michael, the human resources manager, to come to his office to discuss an urgent matter.

They scheduled a three o'clock meeting in his office to discuss this petition. Michael was very empathetic, and he'd known Zilas for about fifteen years. Michael expressed his concerns as well as a solution to this petition.

"Neither your position or Zilas's is in jeopardy for dismissal due to an old policy about relatives," Michael stated. "The policy has been revised, and if we were to let you go, we would have to dismiss all of the hospital because there are plenty of relatives working here—and some even in the same department. Please disregard the petition and continue doing a great job."

"Thank you so much for your assistance with this matter, Michael," Kanasia replied.

She walked away with her head held high, accompanied by a smile on her face.

The week went so fast with all the worrying about Zilas and the unnecessary confusion and conflict at work. It was now Friday, November 5, 1987. As Kanasia sat at her desk to prepare for another day of work, Ruth walked in.

"I want to apologize to you for the other day," she said.

"Get out of my office now. I don't accept your apology," Kanasia softly but sternly informed her.

Ruth worked with her head down, her faced filled with sadness. Kanasia didn't care, because she caused her hurt and embarrassment, inconvenienced her and her family, and caused conflict in her office. Kanasia never wanted to see her face again, because of all the problems she created.

At nine thirty that morning, Zilas's doctor came to see Kanasia in her office. He requested that they go somewhere private to discuss Zilas's condition. She followed Dr. Pellagrino to the psychiatric unit, as this was a safe place to discuss a personal issue, because the people in the hospital were afraid to go over there. When they reached the psychiatric unit, they went into the conference room. Dr. Pellagrino began to inquire about Kanasia and the girls.

"How are you and your daughters doing?"

Kanasia told him about all the rumors and complications that they were encountering, especially at work. As she conversed with Dr. Pellagrino, she could see a cloud of doom floating in the air around them. She knew there was something bad going on with Zilas for him to come to her office and not wait until she reached the hospital where Zilas was.

Dr. Pellagrino began to explain to her that Zilas had a very weak immune system that was not functioning properly. This caused him to have a difficult time fighting off any colds, pneumonia, or infections. Dr. Pellagrino also informed Kanasia that an HIV test was conducted and the results for Zilas came back positive. Zilas had the AIDS virus.

Kanasia froze as if in shock. She couldn't even believe what Dr. Pellagrino just told her. She couldn't feel her legs or feet, and her palms began to grow cold and sweaty. Her heart was pounding like a bongo being hit with a triple beat, and her voice began to fade into hoarseness.

"What about me and the girls?" Kanasia cried.

Dr. Pellagrino hugged her and told her to come into his office to be tested. They arranged for the girls to go to their pediatrician to be tested.

As she looked away from him during their conversation, Dr. Pellagrino became concerned. "Mrs. Drummond, are you okay?"

"Yes," she replied. "How did Zilas get HIV? Can we kiss, touch, or have intercourse?" she inquired. "I have so many questions right now, and I don't know what to do."

Dr. Pellagrino informed her that casual contact was okay, but he insisted that Kanasia get some type of counseling and therapy sessions to find out more information on this illness. Dr. Pellagrino and Kanasia ended their discussion, and she informed him that she would seek therapy and get the girls and herself tested.

Kanasia began to walk back to her office. Every step made her feel as if she were floating aimlessly. She felt cold and emotionally drained. Kanasia approached her office trying her best to look calm, but as soon as no one was in the office, she broke down and began to cry.

As she was weeping, one of her transporters walked in and saw her crying. "Mrs. Drummond, are you all right?" Megan asked.

The room was filled with horrifying grief. Continuous tears rolled off her face to the floor. Kanasia cried so much that the front of her dress was wet. She decided to confide in Megan and informed her of what the doctor just said. At this point, she felt it didn't matter since the word was out that Zilas had AIDS anyway. Megan hugged Kanasia and consoled her while the tears continued to flow. She pulled herself together and told Megan that she was going to go see Zilas at the hospital.

Kanasia left her job in tears, but she wanted to see what kind of mood Zilas was in. She headed toward the hospital where he was. It wasn't visiting hours yet, but she was allowed to go up to see him early, likely due to the new diagnosis.

As she approached his room, she noticed that he was crying just as much. His frail body began to resemble the AIDS patients she had seen on the television. She couldn't picture anything but him dying from this disease. She imagined herself and the girls being left alone. Just as the outside was cloudy, gloomy, and dreary, so were their emotions. This was worse than dealing with her mother's stroke. It was as if a death sentence was just imposed upon Zilas—and possibly Kanasia since she was intimate with Zilas. After all, he was her husband. She loved him, and she knew he never wanted this to happen.

Kanasia was in a trance as she watched him curled up in a fetal position, crying like a baby. She consoled him, but so many thoughts and questions were running through her head. "Honey, how do you think you got this"? Teary eyed Zilas looked at Kanasia and said, 'I believe it was from a needlestick from one of the patients I took care of at the emergency room at my second job." She felt like her head was going to explode. Kanasia wondered why this had to happen to them and why those rumors had to be true.

She was disgusted with God because she felt she was losing another person she loved to sickness or death. Kanasia was afraid that Zilas would attempt suicide with this diagnosis because he was such an independent man who loved to work and hated to be down in any way.

She grabbed Zilas tighter in her arms and told him, "Honey, everything is going to be okay. We'll get through this!"

"Honey, sell the car and house. Take care of yourself and the girls," Zilas said.

"We are not going to sell anything, Zilas. I love you no matter what!" Kanasia replied.

When Zilas asked her why she wasn't at work, she told him that she came as soon as Dr. Pellagrino told her about his condition.

"I needed to see you, be with you, and hold you in my arms!"

Zilas encouraged Kanasia to go home and take care of the girls and her mother. He told her that he would be okay. "Please don't tell anyone about my disease except my brother Mark," Zilas insisted. Kanasia tearfully agreed, hugged him, and proceeded for home.

13

Kanasia left the hospital still in a trance from the diagnosis. She opened the car door and began to drive toward the parkway to home. She was driving eighty miles per hour and was not even aware of it until she almost hit another car. Kanasia felt as if she were in a bad nightmare that she couldn't wake up from. As she was driving along the parkway, a song came on the radio by Regina Belle, entitled "So Many Tears." The lyrics filled the car with the emotions she was experiencing.

"And I don't even pray anymore at night, 'cause I don't think that anyone hears. All that is heard when it's late at night are my tears, are my tears, so many tears, so many tears!" she sang as the tears rolled uncontrollably.

When she arrived home, her mind was roaming all over the place thinking about Zilas, the kids, her mother, the house, and Zilas's car. All the things they'd worked so hard to accomplish were falling apart. The thought of being alone to care for her children and mother was swallowing her up.

Kanasia had a daily ritual of questioning God and asking him *why*? Her faith fell far, far behind, but Samantha always encouraged her to keep pushing on.

"Kanasia, don't give up. The Lord will make a way," her mother stated with a glowing, uplifting smile.

She decided it was time to inform Zilas's brother Mark about the AIDS, so she called him and asked him to come over. Mark refused to come and insisted that she just tell him over the telephone. Kanasia was upset when Mark refused to come over, so she insisted he go see his brother at the hospital today and that he needed him now. Kanasia threw the phone.

Her blood was boiling over from the lack of brotherly support. Kanasia had not informed her mother yet about Zilas having AIDS. It was very hard keeping this a secret, especially from Samantha. Kanasia attempted to put the telephone call with Mark behind her and focus on the girls. She walked upstairs and tightly embraced her children and mother.

"Da-da," blurted out Charlotte.

This was the first time she called for Zilas. The tears began to stream down Kanasia's face. She wished he were home to hear her say his name for the first time. But through all the bad times, her children could always turn a horrible day into a fun day and make her feel so much better.

Since Zilas was diagnosed with AIDS, Kanasia's appetite was nonexistent. She lost fifteen pounds, and every night she tossed and turned in bed, staring aimlessly at the ceiling tiles. Her happiness was gone. She felt her world was out of control, spinning around like a globe. She would try to stay calm and relax by listening to music, but not even that was comforting to her anymore.

Kanasia was so restless that Samantha would hear her walking the floors all night long after the girls were asleep. "Kanasia, come here," her mother called out one night. "Baby, what's wrong?"

She tried to hold it in, but she couldn't keep the horrible news in anymore. If Kanasia couldn't confide in her mother, then she couldn't confide in anyone. She sat on her bed, breaking down, and began to tell her about Zilas having AIDS. She told her mother that she and the girls would have to be tested for it. Samantha's face was shocked, and she was left briefly speechless.

Kanasia began to tell her that she didn't hate Zilas or blame him for contracting AIDS, but she did feel that she and her girls were doomed. She didn't want them to become orphans.

This AIDS was like a death sentence, and everyone she heard about that came down with it died. There was no recovery from it but death. Kanasia was afraid that she might come down with it since it was a disease that was spread through sexual contact, blood, and bodily fluids.

As she released this news to her mother, she began to feel like a balloon that was full of air but suddenly the air rapidly escaped until it was flat. Kanasia told Samantha that Zilas didn't want anyone outside their home or family to know about the virus, so she made her promise not to tell their family, her friends, or her nursing assistant. Kanasia stressed the importance of keeping this a secret due to the potential discrimination.

Samantha agreed, but her face was sad. "Um, um, um!" was all she could utter. Just at that moment Kanasia remembered a heated disagreement she had with her mother before she and Zilas married. In this disagreement Samantha blurted out, "something is wrong with his blood"! Kanasia all of a sudden realized her mother had experienced a déjà vu at that time. The very words her mother stated came true four years later

She grabbed Kanasia's hand, and they prayed and read Scriptures together. Samantha also told Kanasia to tell Zilas to do the same so they could build up the strength to deal with this situation.

Kanasia left Samantha's room, and she went to call Zilas to see if Mark called or came to see him.

"No. Honey, I'll talk to you later," Zilas replied, and he hung up the telephone. She was hurt that Zilas didn't want to talk, but she could understand his mood. She called him later that night to make sure he was okay.

It had now been four weeks since Zilas was hospitalized, but he was receiving AZT antiviral medication that was used to treat AIDS. This was good to know because Kanasia hoped he would be coming home soon. She still remained confused, distraught but she never ever questioned Zilas's explanation for contracting HIV or interrogated him any further. She accepted it and dismissed any previous speculations about Zilas's sexual practices or recreational drug use. Kanasia's main focus now was to keep her family together, continue loving her husband unconditionally, help him cope, provide as much normalcy as possible, and maintain their assets to avoid losing what they worked hard to achieve.

Before Zilas came home, she made appointments for herself and the girls at the lab to be tested. Samantha had a doctor's appointment scheduled for this same week. Zilas, Samantha, and Kanasia all had the same internal medicine doctor, Dr. Pellagrino, so while Samantha had her appointment, Kanasia had her blood drawn.

The doctor informed her that it would take about three to four weeks to get the results back. As her mother was finishing her appointment, she stood to walk into the waiting room, when she suddenly became weak and fell on the floor. She looked like she was having a stroke again.

"Mom! Mom, are you okay?" Kanasia screamed out for help from the doctor and staff at the office.

Dr. Pellagrino took her pulse and blood pressure readings, but her mother was rapidly becoming incoherent. The office staff called an ambulance to take her to the hospital for further evaluation.

Kanasia's luck was shot. Everyone was getting sick, and now Zilas and her mother were in the hospital.

"Oh my God, how much more can I take?" she cried out on her knees.

It was difficult now because she had to rely on the babysitter to watch the girls longer so she could spend time with Zilas and her mother at the hospital. The only good thing was that Samantha was an inpatient at the hospital where Kanasia worked, so this made it easier to see her without abiding by the visitors' schedule. A lab test, electrocardiogram, and an angiogram were conducted to find out what was going on with Samantha.

The following week, Kanasia took the girls to the lab to have their blood drawn, and she dreaded it. It was a horrible experience for them due to the needles that had to be inserted into their veins. They were so young to be dealing with this, and they didn't know what was going on. Kanasia tried her best to explain what the procedure was, and the lab technician was very kind and empathetic.

Shannon's blood was drawn first. Kanasia held her hand as the lab technician began to place the needle into her vein. Shannon began to cry.

"No, no! Stop it; it hurts!" she screamed.

"Squeeze my hand as tightly as you can, Shannon. I's almost finished," Kanasia said in a soothing voice. Kanasia gave her a big hug and kiss.

Then it was Charlotte's turn. This was going to be more difficult because she was still an infant. Kanasia held Charlotte in her lap, and the lab technician tried to play a game with Charlotte to ease the tension, but she was resistant to a stranger touching her. All of a sudden, Charlotte began to scream, holler, and squirm around in her arms, accompanied by some strong kicks and arm thrusts. Kanasia tried her best to console her and calm her down, but Charlotte wasn't having it. The next thing she knew, Charlotte kicked the lab technician in her breast.

"Oh my God, I'm so sorry. Are you okay?" Kanasia asked.

She was understanding and walked away for a few minutes to allow Charlotte to calm down. After five minutes passed, Charlotte calmed down, so they tried again. This time around, Kanasia had to restrain Charlotte so they could get it over with. She began to scream and wiggle again, but the lab technician was able to get her blood successfully this time. Kanasia hated this and felt they never should have been exposed to this torture. But due to their father, this had to be done so they knew where they all stood with this disease.

The next day, Samantha's test results were back, and she was diagnosed with a blockage in her arteries causing atherosclerosis. She was treated with blood thinners, cholesterol, and heart medication called Digoxin. Samantha gradually began to feel better, and she was scheduled to return home by the following week.

Trouble erupted again in the hospital where Kanasia worked. Vicious rumors started again, and this time it involved her mother. The employees started saying her mother had AIDS too, because she had been on the floor in the hospital where the AIDS patients were. The rumor escalated into all of them having AIDS.

This time around, Kanasia could laugh at the stupidity circulating around the hospital. But the atmosphere in her office became worse. Her staff would leave a full box of alcohol prep pads as well as a box of disposable gloves on the desk. They began to throw out her pens every time one of them had to answer the telephone after her. All of these things made Kanasia feel hurt, as if she were poison, and she hated being treated that way.

She was so upset that she left the office to go to the bathroom. As she returned, she witnessed one of the workers cleaning down the desk chair with alcohol and throwing Kanasia's pen in the garbage. This was the first time she had actually witnessed it occurring. The worker clearly didn't know she would come back so fast from the bathroom, and Kanasia stood there watching her, but she couldn't even speak. She just watched as the worker's face became red, her eyes dilated, and she stood there motionless and speechless. Her face was soiled with guilt as she tried to explain why she was cleaning.

"My hands were itching so I cleaned everything down!" she professed.

Kanasia didn't respond to her lies, and she asked her to move so she could sit back down in her seat.

She tried her best not to show her anger, but Kanasia was mad as hell. Eventually, the madness passed, and through prayer and Scriptures, she became a stronger woman. She learned how to deal with their ignorance and disrespectful behavior. The ordeal transformed her from a twenty-one-year-old young lady into a woman.

14

It was now time for Zilas to come home from the hospital. He was off the oxygen and feeling better. He was fragile, and it was frightening having him home because all Kanasia could do was picture how he left home gasping for air. She felt so incompetent and vulnerable, but it was great to have him back home with her and the girls. He was still very weepy, and he sat in the living room for a while before going upstairs to their bedroom. His cheekbones were sunken in, and his clothes were swallowing him up.

Samantha was discharged from the hospital the day before Thanksgiving. Kanasia was glad that they were back home where they belonged, especially for the holiday. Samantha also arrived home weak, and Kanasia was having a difficult time assisting her upstairs to her bedroom. Zilas had been standing in the kitchen looking embarrassed, and he didn't eagerly come out to greet her mother when they arrived. However, when he discovered that Kanasia was having a hard time getting her up the stairs, he ran to their rescue. The embarrassment vanished quickly, and the smiles and conversations began.

The next week, Kanasia called Dr. Pellagrino's office for her HIV results. She began to tremble. Her hands were drenched in perspiration like a tray of ice cubes left out and dripping everywhere, and her heart was beating like a drum. It took Dr. Pellagrino about fifteen minutes to come to the telephone, but he eventually answered.

"Mrs. Drummond, your test results were negative, and you do not have HIV!" he said.

Kanasia was relieved and began thanking God. She hung up the telephone and called the girls' pediatrician to find out their test results. Dr. Davis answered the telephone and began to review the lab results.

"Mrs. Drummond, Shannon and Charlotte are okay and are negative for HIV."

Great news in the same day.

"Praise God!" Kanasia yelled out. She was relieved and the burden of worry lifted. She had a glass of red wine to celebrate this good news. She still felt bad for Zilas because his diagnosis was like a death sentence. She told him and Samantha that she and the girls were negative for HIV. They were both were relieved that they were not infected.

Now they could settle back down as a family and try to go back to normalcy.

Zilas was still unable to do anything strenuous around the house, so Kanasia took on his chores of sweeping the exterior of the house, shoveling snow, keeping water in the furnace, and making sure there was enough oil in the tank. Little by little, he began to do more things around the house. Kanasia tried to persuade Zilas to take it easy and relax, but he didn't listen, so she stopped trying to convince him not to do anything around the house. She allowed it because this was therapy to him, and it made him feel like a man again.

Zilas was sanding the wood floors in the foyer, living room, and dining room, and then he applied the polyurethane. Those wood floors were beautiful and shined so much that they looked like glass. Kanasia was afraid to walk on the floors because they looked slippery. He received so many compliments on the floors from family and friends that visited them. But throughout these visits, Zilas would always wear his bathrobe to conceal the real weight loss underneath, and he didn't take off the bathrobe until the visitors left. Zilas and Kanasia sat down and talked about everything as much as possible, and she encouraged him that he would be okay.

Kanasia kept everything as normal as possible around the house. They both slept in the same bed, used the same bathroom, used the same eating utensils, and she never discriminated against him in any way. They still had sex, but now they used a condom, and they utilized safe sex practices. She loved her husband, and she was not going to deny him pleasure.

Kanasia was convinced that he loved her and the girls and did not want anything to happen to them. She was afraid of contracting the disease the first time they made love, but she reassured herself that as long as they practiced safe sex and continued testing, she should be okay. The first time they had sex, Zilas became sick from the motion, but they enjoyed each other and vowed to always use a condom when engaged in sexual activities.

At the end of January in 1988, Zilas was ready to go back to work. He went to Dr. Pellagrino for his return to work physical and note. When he went back to his job, the employees were stunned because he'd gained his weight back and was looking great. They thought he wouldn't be able to work again, because of his AIDS, but he fooled them all. Kanasia and Zilas sat back and laughed at all those doubters.

As Zilas walked into the hospital, the employees would stop and stare in amazement. He and Kanasia ate lunch together in the cafeteria every time they worked. All eyes were on them, and as they walked the corridors, whispers of gossip echoed the halls.

They would say, "I wonder if she has it too. How can they let him come back in here to work with that?"

They would hear all these comments, ignore them, and keep walking. It was hard for Zilas to watch his coworkers and other employees around the hospital change toward him. People he thought were his friends no longer wanted to associate with him. This hurt him tremendously, but he learned to adjust, just as Kanasia did. Among the negative, mean-hearted, and spiteful ones were a few dedicated, sincere friends. As time went on, Zilas began to adapt and started visiting his friends again.

Zilas was adjusting to being back at home, working, and taking his pentamidine treatments at the clinic every two weeks. This medication helped kill the organism that caused infections and treat the pneumocystis pneumonia, the lung infection associated with AIDS, but it had nasty side effects like nausea, vomiting, dizziness, and diarrhea. On the day of his treatments, he would be very weak and tired.

Kanasia felt happy that he was adapting to his routine and looked healthy again. But within six to eight months, Zilas began having mental changes that consisted of memory loss. He was unreasonable, difficult to deal with, argumentative, and difficult to communicate with at times.

Then he began hanging out with his friends so much that he didn't have time for Kanasia and their daughters. She was at home every night with the same routine: cooking, eating, bathing the girls, entertaining the girls, and waiting for Zilas to return home.

Kanasia was so bored on her weekends off that it depressed her. Things were better at the office now, and many people that had aggravated her or wanted her to leave ended up resigning or being terminated. This made the work environment much more comfortable, and she began to socialize with some of her staff outside of the job. It was a lot of fun. They went to the beach, bars, movies, dinner, dancing clubs, and even went on a weekend cruise. Kanasia was enjoying herself with or without Zilas being around.

Nevertheless, despite Kanasia having a good time, she would still worry about contracting HIV, and this thought always dangled in her mind. She became so obsessed that she had a discussion with Zilas and informed him that she wanted to have her fallopian tubes tied and burned. Kanasia decided that she did not want to chance bringing another child into the world and risk infecting him or her.

She typed a letter and had Zilas sign it, giving her his consent to have her tubes tied. Kanasia took it to her gynecologist, and they began to prepare for the procedure. Zilas was sad about her decision, but he knew this was the right thing to do.

Kanasia felt that as black people, they had enough struggles, but the last thing she wanted to do was unexpectedly end up pregnant. Sometimes her emotions would change, and she would get angry with Zilas for exposing her and their daughters to HIV, as well as all of the harassment and discrimination they had to endure.

She especially felt angry when he would ignore them and go around partying, getting high with his friends, and go on with his life as if nothing ever happened.

His personality and conduct were drastically changing toward them in a negative way. Kanasia began to crave someone she could talk to, hang out with, and try to escape all the madness she was encountering with Zilas. She was tired of feeling blue, lonely, and disregarded by Zilas. Zilas was no longer the loving, considerate man she'd married. He'd turned into a heartless bastard.

Kanasia started hanging out at her office with three of her staff members. This gave her relief from her situation at home with Zilas. Her lonely nights were now filled with drinking and hanging with friends before she came home from work. But Kanasia always took care of her daughters and mother, regardless of how difficult things became at home.

Zilas began regressing from his treatments at the clinic, and his mental changes were increasing. He also started staying home more. He became possessive and jealous of her friends. Zilas began to issue physical threats on Kanasia's life, and he verbalized that he didn't want her talking or hanging out with any of them. Every time she wanted to go out on the weekends and he was supposed to watch the girls, he would deliberately work overtime so she couldn't go.

Along with Zilas changing, so was Kanasia. She was developing into a woman with ideas, decision-making skills, and independence. She no longer just went along with whatever he said or thought about. Kanasia had her own mind and sexuality. Most of all, he made her grow up faster than she could ever have imagined.

15

It was now September. The weather was changing quickly, but they had some more warm days left before fall and then winter rolled in.

Kanasia decided to go out one weekend with Jane from the office. They went to see the famous Chippendale dancers Dancers. They had a blast, and it felt good to get away and have some fun. They got back by midnight.

When Kanasia arrived home, Zilas was fuming with anger. "I'm sick, and you're going out having a ball. You don't give a damn about me!" Zilas uttered.

Kanasia ignored him, laughed, and headed for the bedroom. Zilas followed her upstairs to the bedroom. "If I ever see you or any of your friends on the street going somewhere, I'm going to run all of you over!" he threatened. "If I'm asked what happened by the police, I'll tell them the car malfunctioned." Zilas had a face full of hate.

Kanasia looked at him in amazement. After witnessing his anger, she knew he meant every word coming out of his mouth. "Zilas, I take all the threats that you are expressing very seriously. I am keeping track!" Kanasia screamed at him.

"I'm playing with you," Zilas replied.

"Well, I'm not playing with your ass, and no one threatens me and gets away with it!" she retorted.

To avoid any further conflicts with Zilas, Kanasia began to stay home more. She was under so much stress from Zilas and his new nasty disposition.

In November, she did go out again with Jane. She went out with Jane to visit her Aunt Jeanine's apartment. Kanasia was getting tired of smoking weed and drinking. This was becoming a boring routine for her, so she mentioned to Jane one day that she wanted to try cocaine. That night, her aunt had all the cocaine they needed, and Kanasia quickly started snorting cocaine.

She liked it. Her only complaint was that she couldn't sleep after doing it. She started buying cocaine from a coworker's boyfriend, and she was snorting cocaine, accompanied by a bottle of champagne, at least every two weeks when she got paid.

Kanasia would take care of her mother and daughters by feeding them, bathing them, and putting them to sleep for the night, and then her escapade of snorting and drinking would begin in the comfort of her locked bedroom or attic. She would have a music marathon and listen to all of her records. This was her way of escaping Zilas, AIDS, and all the problems he caused her.

She was becoming obsessed with the cocaine; she had to have a few lines and a glass of wine before even going to work. Her attitude was changing for the worse. She would verbally attack anyone at any opportunity. Kanasia no longer gave a damn, and when she didn't have cocaine, she would substitute it for marijuana, alcohol, or mescaline. She was in her own world and didn't want anyone or anything to interfere with it.

Zilas was hanging out again with his friends. He would get high off marijuana and angel dust and drink alcohol, so Kanasia took advantage of this by entertaining herself. After a while, she was able to ignore Zilas and act as if everything were normal. They were both enjoying themselves, but they both felt miserable without the drugs.

One night Kanasia was so disgusted with the whole disease thing that she snorted twenty lines of cocaine in a matter of two minutes. Her heart began to race, her throat became dry, and she began to have chills. Kanasia was frightened, and she began to pace back and forth to get warm. She was fearful that she wouldn't wake up if she lay down, so she attempted to drink a glass of water.

Zilas was still hanging out with his friends, but when he arrived home two hours later, Kanasia was so glad to see him that she cuddled him like a teddy bear. This incident made her cool it with the cocaine, but her drinking continued.

It was approaching the Christmas season, and they had a few friends over at the house to bring in the holidays. While Zilas was smoking marijuana, Kanasia had her cocaine to comfort herself. Zilas was aware of it, and he snorted some with her too, but he wasn't impressed with it, so he continued to smoke marijuana.

In February, Kanasia and Zilas began to have problems again. This time, he was becoming obsessed with the thought of leaving Kanasia, the kids, the house, and his car behind. He was frightened and frightening to live with. Every day was a new issue. It was getting more stressful in the house, with constant arguments, rampages of anger, and the constant complaining of anything and everything. He complained that the girls were making too much noise or the stereo or television was too loud.

Zilas coughed all night long, and he began to start cutting off his friends and family, going into isolation. His energy, appetite, and sensitivity toward their family was decreasing. If anything made Kanasia stop doing drugs, it was this. She needed to be strong and clearheaded to deal with this next bout of changes that Zilas was experiencing. He was getting out of control with wanting the house totally quiet to the point where if girls were in their rooms playing, Zilas would suddenly yell at them.

"Shannon, if that noise doesn't stop, I will throw you down the stairs!" he threatened one time.

Kanasia ran downstairs to the dining room where he was sitting, and she screamed back at him. "Calm your ass down!"

She checked on Samantha, and Kanasia told her that she was going to take the girls out to Burger King for a while in order to get away from him for an hour or two. Shannon and Charlotte were crying hysterically.

"What's wrong with Daddy? Why does he want to hurt us?" they said.

Kanasia sat them down at Burger King and wiped away their tears. She tried her best to explain to them that their daddy was sick. But even though he was sick, it did not excuse his nasty attitude and threats. They ate, and the girls played in the jungle gym area. They seemed like they were relaxing a little, so they left and returned home.

Zilas was becoming more threatening by refusing to support Kanasia financially. He only wanted her to go to work, the store, and back home. If she stayed out too long, he became erratic and began to accuse her of having a boyfriend. Ironically, she had no one but him in her life.

Things became so frustrating between her and Zilas that she had little desire to have any type of sexual relations with him. He was becoming more evil and hateful. She was afraid to do anything with him. Her trust in him was decreasing little by little. Zilas was persistent to have sex with her, and he began to have problems holding an erection. He became frustrated and so did Kanasia. After about two unsuccessful attempts to have sex, their sexual relationship gradually ended. She feared that he would puncture the condom and she would end up infected too. Zilas was so obsessed with having sex with her that Kanasia felt like he was on a mission to infect her.

Zilas believed that everything he said was right and should not be disputed. He tried to take revenge on every person that caused problems for them during his illness. There were times he wouldn't even talk to Kanasia. He was declining physically.

All of this was making life unbearable, depressing, and frustrating for Kanasia. She had to go out to escape the hell at home with him. The days she went to work, she was so sad and would break down and cry. Kanasia's attendance at work began to decline, and she started calling out sick. Before she knew it, all of the mental and verbal abuse physically affected her. She started having problems swallowing and felt as though her throat was closing up.

When Zilas came home from work, Kanasia told him that she wanted to go to the emergency room to be looked at. He looked at her and didn't respond. Kanasia asked him if he would come with her.

"I guess so," he responded.

She was hurt that he was acting as if he didn't care about her. They went to the hospital. Luckily, it was rather empty, so Kanasia was able to see the doctor right away. She explained her swallowing problems to the doctor, so he examined her throat, but he couldn't find anything wrong. He suggested that Kanasia gargle warm water and salt for the irritation.

They went back home, and Kanasia did as the doctor told her. She physically felt better, but she was mentally ripped apart. Her psychological state was in disarray, her nerves were bad, and she was restless, which led to constant insomnia. She went into her mother's room and fell asleep on her bed. Kanasia began to feel better as she rested there. She was on an emotional roller coaster on a downward spiral, but she tried her best to go on with life for the sake of her daughters and Samantha.

16

It was March, and Kanasia was preparing to surprise Shannon for her fifth birthday party. On March 7, Kanasia took the day off work and dropped the girls off at the babysitter's house. However, Zilas was angry that she missed work that day. She felt he was being unreasonable, and he didn't even say if he would join them at her babysitter's for the party. He was angry and verbally nasty to her. Kanasia ignored him because she wanted Shannon to have a great birthday party.

Kanasia proceeded to get her hair done, but as she was leaving the beauty parlor, she noticed that the car was acting up. It felt shaky and wobbly while she was driving, but the only thing on her mind was picking up the cake and driving to Shannon's babysitter's house. As she drove through Branch Brook Park in Newark to pick up the cake, the car became more and more unstable. She began to worry when the car made a loud *thump, thump, squeak* sound. Right before her eyes, the front tire on the passenger's side of the car began to roll in front of her on the road. It was as if an inexperienced bowler had thrown a bowling ball swiftly down the lane. Kanasia was terrified. "What the hell is going on?" Kanasia screamed.

She managed to slow the car down and stop it. She got out and examined the car, but she was shaking like a leaf. She had never been so close to death before.

"Thank God no one was behind me and I wasn't going that fast," she said aloud. A car finally came up behind her, and the man stopped to ask Kanasia if she was okay.

"Can I help you, miss?" the driver said with concern in his voice.

Kanasia took the driver up on his offer to drop her off at the mechanic, which was nearby. She told Jack, the mechanic, what happened, and he sent a tow truck to recover the car from the park.

Kanasia called Zilas at work to tell him what happened with the car, but she was unable to reach him, so she left a message with his supervisor. She then proceeded to call her mother. She told Samantha what happened and inquired whether Zilas was home yet.

"No, Kanasia, he's not here, but when he comes in, I'll tell him to pick you up at the babysitter's."

"Thank you, Mom," Kanasia replied.

She waited until the car arrived at the shop and the mechanic examined the car. He found that the front tire on the passenger side had been altered. The rim was welded down, which caused the tire to not adhere to the rim. This made it become dislodged and fall off.

"In all my twelve years of working as a mechanic, I haven't seen anything like this," he said. Jack showed her what he was referring to and the damage left behind. "Mrs. Drummond, you are lucky that you weren't killed today!"

As he spoke, Kanasia became very frightened. She left the car for the mechanic to fix, and she walked to the bakery to get the cake. From the bakery, Kanasia took a cab to the girls' babysitter's house. When she arrived, she was still shaken up. Kanasia wanted her to have a good birthday, so she played it off and tried to remain calm for Shannon's sake.

Zilas finally arrived, and as they walked toward his car, Kanasia began to tell him about what happened to the car. She noticed that he had no verbal reaction, but he had a display of anger on his face.

When they were halfway home, he finally responded. "You keep calling out sick from work. You call out every week. You're going to get fired! I heard the administration is talking about getting rid of you and closing your whole department down!" he yelled.

Kanasia wondered what was going on. She was almost killed today, and all Zilas could think about was her calling out sick from work. She was in a twilight zone. Her husband wasn't even concerned about whether she was okay or worried about the car.

"If you become unemployed, we're selling this house!" he exclaimed.

Kanasia was now furious and burning up with resentment for him. She began thinking that he had a connection to the problems with her car that day. "If I get fired from my job, it's no big deal! I'm tired of the pressure that I am under at work and home, and dammit, something has got to give!" she screamed at the top of her lungs.

Kanasia told Zilas that he was not her supervisor, her job was none of his business, and he should worry about his own employment.

When they entered the house, Kanasia took the girls upstairs to their rooms. She stuck her head in her mother's room to let her know she was home safely.

Kanasia then proceeded to the telephone to call Jack to see when the car would be ready. She asked him if he thought the tire was tampered with. All he told her was that this was heavy metal, and throughout all the rolling of the tire dislodgment, the bolts remained in place.

"I have never seen a rim bent like that. This is weird," Jack said.

The details of the tire assessment, Zilas's attitude, and his reactions became an unwanted revelation.

Kanasia and her mother began discussing, and she told Kanasia to be careful around Zilas. "Kanasia, something is definitely wrong with the situation that occurred today," her mother said.

Kanasia was so terrified, and she began asking herself, "Why? Why does he hate me so much? Or is this all about his collecting on my life insurance policy?"

All she could think about was the tire rolling in front of the car as she was driving. That's when Kanasia realized God was with her; she could have been killed or critically injured. One particular Scripture from the Old Testament in the King James version came to mind in the book of Isaiah chapter 54, verse 17: "No weapon that is formed against thee shall prosper." Kanasia began to thank God for his protection and the miracle of surviving the horrible accident. He saved her life from hurt, harm, danger, and possible death.

As the night progressed, she attended to her daughters and mother by preparing dinner and baths. She placed the girls in bed and returned to her room for bed.

The day after Shannon's birthday, Kanasia arose to prepare the girls for the day. Zilas was getting ready for work. He was very quiet and didn't look or talk to Kanasia. He then slammed a twenty-dollar bill on the dresser.

"Take a cab to get to the girls' babysitter's and then take a bus to work," Zilas said in a nasty tone.

He didn't even offer Kanasia or their daughters a ride in his car. She was so angry and frustrated with all the events that occurred within the last twenty-four hours that she decided to declare her marriage null and void. When she arrived at work, she threw her wedding ring and engagement ring in the trash can. As the day went on Kanasia calmed down, removed rings from the trash can, cleaned them, and placed them back on her finger.

Kanasia later called the mechanic. The car would be ready at three o'clock, so Kanasia went to pick it up at the end of the workday.

As March went on, Kanasia continued to get more into her prayers and Bible reading, and she began to attend a local church. Her daughters and mother had a nightly ritual of praying together before bed. This really helped to destress the atmosphere in the house.

As April approached, Zilas and the house were peaceful. It was so peaceful that it was scary because Zilas was back to being his normal self. He was talking normally, laughing, and being cooperative again.

His birthday was here, and Kanasia decided to make him a seafood dinner with cheesecake for dessert. Zilas enjoyed the meal, but she could tell his depression was sinking back in again. Kanasia tried to talk him out of the mood and gave him a big hug.

There was a weird feeling in the air around the house. It was peaceful, but not quite comfortable considering all the changes that Kanasia and Zilas were going through. It felt as if something bad was going to happen. This feeling caused Kanasia to be restless, sleepless at night, and depressed.

Her birthday was here now, and she went to work as usual, feeling kind of down because she had no plans of celebration. Zilas didn't say anything about them celebrating, but he did send her a beautiful bouquet of roses. She went on with her workday, and at three o'clock, one of her staff members, Kira, asked Kanasia if she wanted to go to her house for a drink after work. Kanasia went with her because she had no other plans. Zilas was picking the girls up from the babysitter's, so she had enough time to hang out for a little bit.

However, after arriving at Kira's house, Kanasia realized she was acting strange. Kira left Kanasia at her house and went out to run an errand. Kanasia wondered what was going on. It was getting dark, and she decided that she needed to go home now. As she was about to leave Kira's house, Kira returned home. When Kanasia told Kira that she was leaving, Kira insisted on coming home with her, so they left together.

As Kanasia pulled up in front of the house, everything was dark. She placed the key in the front door, and when she opened it, suddenly she heard people shouting "Surprise!"

The lights came on, and Zilas, the girls, her mother, Paris, Orain, Eddie, friends, and her coworkers were standing there. She was shocked to see so many people there to celebrate her birthday. She was also surprised to know that Zilas had prepared everything from the decorations to the food, champagne, music, and guests. Kanasia was so happy and speechless. All she could think about was that she had the best husband in the whole world. She knew Zilas really loved her and that he didn't mind letting the world know it. It was the best birthday surprise she ever had in her life.

Later that night, Zilas told her that he wanted to give her a surprise birthday party for her twenty-fourth birthday because he didn't know if he would be around for her twenty-fifth. Kanasia began to cry, and she hugged Zilas tightly. "Thank you so much. I love you very much," she whispered in his ear.

Even after the party ended, Kanasia was still walking around on cloud nine. But throughout her home, there was still a strange feeling in the air. She couldn't pinpoint it, but Zilas was quiet, peaceful, and humble at home every night, without any complaints or attitudes. However, Zilas stared at Kanasia all the time with a cold look on his face.

17

The next week, they were back to their weekly routine around the house and work. Kanasia came home from work to find Zilas sitting in the bedroom. He told her that he had an appointment with another doctor about his illness, and she was located in the next town Monroe. He explained that this doctor was not a medical doctor but a spiritualist. She dealt with spirits, and she told him she could cure him of AIDS. When Zilas told Kanasia this, she didn't quite understand the details involved in this visit to the doctor. She was imagining that Zilas was going to see one of those five-dollar palm readers with a crystal ball.

"How do you feel about me going to visit one of these doctors?" Zilas asked.

"I'm uncertain, but maybe she could help you."

"Please do not tell your mother that I am going to see a spiritualist," Zilas begged.

She told him she wouldn't mention it to her.

The next day, Zilas went to see Dr. Diaz, the spiritual doctor. He left early in the morning and didn't return home until eight thirty that night. When Zilas arrived, he was coughing and vomiting for hours. The doctor had given him a bag full of items such as herbs, incense, and a list of things he needed to buy, such as white candles, white carnations, white towels, and clear drinking glasses. He was also supposed to get some holy water from a Catholic Church, along with a set of rosary beads.

"Zilas, what happened at your appointment?" Kanasia asked.

Zilas told Kanasia that the doctor said he was cursed with AIDS because of bad things his mother did to other people. She slept with married men and bore their children. The doctor also told Zilas that their home was possessed with the spirit from the previous owner. This woman wanted her house back from their "nigger asses." Kanasia began to tremble, and her heart fluttered.

Zilas told her, "I need to set up an altar in the attic of the house, burn this incense she gave me, perform a ritual to cure myself, and chase this woman's spirit out of our house. You can help me too if you want, honey! Through this white witchcraft, I will cure myself of AIDS."

Kanasia knew Zilas was getting desperate and afraid to die. She tossed and turned all night. Her nerves were so bad that she had to get up to use the bathroom every twenty minutes. She knew more than ever before that her days of drinking and drugging were over now. Life was already turning into a horror movie that she didn't want to be a part of.

On April 20, Kanasia got herself ready for work and then got the girls ready for the day. Zilas didn't go to work on this day, which was odd for him since he didn't call out from work a lot. As she dressed, he kept watching her to the point where she felt very uncomfortable and wondered what was going on in his mind.

At ten thirty that morning Zilas called Kanasia at work to ask her about a radio they had and where it was. She told him and he hung up. Kanasia was sitting at her desk feeling very uncomfortable. At noon, her mother called her saying she smelled smoke.

"Where is Zilas?" Kanasia asked.

"I don't know. I keep calling him, but I think he left the house!" her mother said.

As they talked, Kanasia began to hear *beep, beep, beep.* The smoke detector was going off. Kanasia told her that she was on her way, call 911, and get to the sunporch to safety." But Samantha nervously told Kanasia," I can't my legs are weak"! Kanasia instructed her mother to open the window at the end her bed so she could get air. As she ran out of the hospital to her car, she became short of breath, her heart pounding like a drum. She thought her heart was going to jump out of her chest from fear and nervousness. Kanasia jumped on the highway, and she was home in less than fifteen minutes.

As she approached the sunporch, thick clouds of smoke were billowing through the air and a strong burning smell was coming through the French doors. Smoke surrounded the entire first floor and rose rapidly to the second floor. Kanasia raced upstairs to her mother's room, not stopping until she saw her face. When Kanasia reached her room, she saw Samantha sitting by the open window at the end of her bed, gasping for air with a frightened look in her eyes. Kanasia took her mother downstairs to her car for safety and as they were approaching the sunporch the fire trucks sirens were echoing loudly in front of the house.

There was smoke all over the house now, but no flames were visible. Kanasia knew the smoke was coming from the kitchen, but she was so afraid that she never investigated. She just wanted her mother safe and out of the smoky house.

The fire department arrived, and they headed straight into the kitchen. There they found a big pot with the remains of collard greens from last night's dinner on the stove. They were turned on high until they burned. Zilas was nowhere to be found, but he was definitely the cause of the smoke that could have cost Samantha's life and the destruction of their home.

Kanasia was angry. All she could think about was Zilas visiting this so-called doctor and how this was a conspiracy to kill Samantha, spare his own life, and get them out of the house so he could practice his rituals without interruptions.

One thing after another. Kanasia couldn't believe this was happening. No wonder Zilas didn't want her to tell Samantha about his appointment with Dr. Diaz.

Kanasia gave Paris a call to inform her of the near fire at their home, and to ask her if they could stay with her for a few days.

"Yes, you all can stay. Oh my God, that is terrible," Paris said.

Kanasia packed clothes for her mother, the girls, and herself. They drove to Nancy's to pick up the girls, and then they left to go to Paris's house. Paris lived with her three children and her boyfriend, Kenny, in a nearby town.

After dropping the girls and Samantha off at Paris's, Kanasia went back by the house at five. Zilas was still not home. She went back to Paris's, and at eight that night, she called the house. Zilas was finally at home. Zilas spoke softly and calmly. He was sounding strange, as if he were under a spell. He asked her what happened at the house today and where they were. He told her that he was getting ready to call the police because he thought someone had hurt them. Kanasia began to scream at him for leaving the pot cooking on the stove and then leaving the house.

"I forgot that the pot was on, and I didn't smell any smoke," Zilas insisted.

She begged him to stop practicing his rituals.

"Honey, I have to continue to cure myself of AIDS, and I want you all to come back home tonight," replied Zilas. "And bring me something to eat when you come back."

"Zilas, I don't know when I'm coming back home!" Kanasia hung up the phone and began to cry.

She attempted to sleep but couldn't. She went back by the house the next morning to get some more clothes, and the house felt spooky, cold, dark, and dreary. The smoke aroma was still lingering in the air from the porch to the inside of the house. Zilas was not there, and Kanasia began to look around. There were signs that he had started practicing his rituals. There was the scent of a lit candle and burned incense.

She approached the last room in the attic. There was an altar set up consisting of Samantha's bureau from her bedroom draped with a white cloth, a Bible, white carnations, a Catholic rite book, and candles. There were dimes scattered all over the floor in the attic and on the porch of the house.

Kanasia was so afraid that she ran out of the house and refused to return without having an escort. When she arrived at work, Zilas began to harass her.

"Honey, are you coming home?"

Zilas's mouth was engraved with a white substance. Around his lips was foamy saliva, and his complexion was gray. He was out of it as though he were hypnotized. Kanasia was so afraid of him that she wouldn't even talk to him. She just walked away. She knew at this point that she did not want to be alone with him anywhere. Kanasia was really starting to fear that he was going to kill her or their whole family.

He was so out of control that the hospital employees were talking about them. Kanasia didn't know what to do or who to talk to. She was nervous, tired, weak, and afraid. Her friends at work would not let her walk around or go to her car by herself. They began to escort her to make sure nothing happened.

18

~~~~~

When Kanasia got home from work, she talked to Paris. Kanasia said that she wanted to go back to the house the next morning so she could get some more of her things. When Kanasia asked Paris if she would come with her, Paris agreed. They went to the babysitter's house first and then to her house.

In the bedroom, there was a Bible on the bed and a white teacup and a saucer filled with water under the bed, along with a list of Zilas's relatives in case of an emergency. The house was cold, dark, and gloomy, surrounded by a peculiar feeling. Kanasia took Paris to see the altar that Zilas set up in the attic.

"He must have lost his mind. This is crazy and scary," Paris said. "Let's get out of here now!"

On the way back to Paris's house, they began to talk about Kanasia's situation. She knew that she needed to reveal more details as to why she and Zilas were having problems.

"Paris, I need to tell you the reason Zilas is acting like this," Kanasia said in a sad voice. "Zilas has AIDS!"

"What?" Paris was clearly shocked, and she sat in silence for a few minutes. "Oh my God, how did he get it? What about you and the kids? This is horrifying news to swallow."

"The girls and I are negative, but I am getting myself tested at least every four to six months to be sure," Kanasia replied.

"I always thought you guys had a great relationship," Paris responded.

"We did have a great relationship until Zilas became sick, and then everything went downhill for us."

"AIDS or no AIDS, Zilas needs to have charges pressed against him for trying to kill Mama. If you don't do it, I'll go to the police station myself," Paris stated. "It's not even safe for you or the rest of the family to be near him right now, and you probably need a restraining order to prevent him from trying to take the girls out of the country. Forget about going home; let's just go to the police station to find out your rights and what you should do to protect yourself."

They went to the local police station, and Kanasia explained the details, from the attempted fire to Zilas's mental condition and having AIDS. The police department told her that she would have to go into the Superior Court in Newark in order to get a restraining order as well as a peace warrant to have Zilas removed from the house and gain her custody of the children. They told her that once Kanasia had the peace warrant, she could come back to the town police department and they would remove Zilas from their home.

Kanasia drove into Newark, went before the judge, and explained everything. She was granted the peace warrant, restraining order, and custody of the girls for one month before a hearing. Kanasia felt bad about doing this, but she felt that Zilas left her with no choice, and Paris's reaction to everything was also scary. Kanasia knew Paris would go to the police if she didn't.

After taking care of that, Kanasia went by the babysitter's to pick up the girls, and she gave Nancy a copy of the custody order. She informed her not to let Zilas pick up the girls if he came for them. Nancy promised her that she would inform Kanasia as well as the police if he tried to come by and get them.

Kanasia took the girls back to Paris's house, and while they felt out of place, they were safe from Zilas. She hated being away from her home, and she hated her breakdown with Paris about Zilas. The thought of relocating her whole family due to all these changes Zilas was going through was scary as hell.

Not only was she suffering; all of them were mentally torn from the separation. Her nerves were so bad that she couldn't sleep, eat, or relax. She didn't even feel comfortable sleeping in her pajamas, so she slept in her jeans. Kanasia's weight began to drop from her lack of appetite. Paris suggested that she go see a doctor to get a checkup and get some medication for her nerves, sleep, and appetite.

While Kanasia was at work, Paris did her own research to make sure that she and her family would not become infected with AIDS since they were in her house. She called the Hyacinth Foundation, which is the national AIDS Foundation that gives information about testing, counselling, and other resources to help patients and their families with AIDS cope with the disease.

When Kanasia arrived back home, Paris had a lot of information to give her about the disease and asked if they ever went to a support meeting.

"No, we have never attended. We were never referred to a support group by the hospital doctors or social worker!" she told her.

"This could really help you and Zilas deal with his illness. This is too much pressure dealing with it by yourself," Paris replied. "I never knew he was sick until now."

The more she discussed this with Paris, the better Kanasia felt inside.

As soon as she felt a little better, she found out that there were rumors circulating around the hospital about threats Zilas was making about their home. One of Kanasia's friends, Darla, called her.

"Zilas had been saying that if you tried to take his house, he was going to burn it down to the ground, even if you were in it. He also said that he was going to take the girls away from you and send them to Antigua so that his relatives can care for them."

Kanasia became more afraid because she knew how much Zilas loved that house; this was not the first time he threatened to do this either. She thought of losing her girls. She always told him he could have his house and she would start over fresh somewhere else.

She hung up with Darla and told Paris about the rumors. Her sister encouraged her to hurry up and go to the police department so she could remove Zilas from the house before something bad really happened. Kanasia was glad that she went to court in time so that Zilas couldn't kidnap her daughters.

Kanasia called her brother Randy and informed him of Zilas having AIDS. She also mentioned that she left him and was living with Paris until things were resolved. Kanasia then requested that Randy come with her to the police department and house to have Zilas removed. Randy agreed. The next day, he picked her up and they went to the police department.

The police came with them back to the house. Kanasia put her key in the door, but it would not open. Zilas had changed all the locks so she couldn't get back in the house. The police began to ring the bell and bang on the door. They ordered Zilas to let them in.

"Mr. Drummond, it's the police. Please open the door now, sir!"

Kanasia could hear Zilas walking down the stairs to open the door.

"What's wrong, Officers?" Zilas asked in a weak and sad voice.

"We have an order to serve you from the court, stating that you must stay away from your wife, kids, and mother-in law. You must also leave the premises now! You have five minutes to gather your clothes and leave the house," ordered one of the police officers.

Randy stood by her side, and Kanasia looked at Zilas with fear in her eyes.

"Why, honey? Why are you having me put out of my own house? I have nowhere to go," Zilas replied.

She told him that she didn't like how he had been acting and the things he said at work.

"Hurry up, Mr. Drummond. You have to leave *now*," one of the officers said in a stern tone.

Zilas finally gathered one bag and approached the porch to leave.

"Where are the keys to the house, Zilas?" Randy asked.

Zilas dug into his pants pocket and handed Kanasia the house keys. His eyes were tearful as he looked at Kanasia with embarrassment glowing on his face. He then got in his car and drove away.

Randy and Kanasia thanked the police for their assistance. They informed them that if they needed anything or had any further problems with Zilas, all they had to do was give them a call. The police left, and Kanasia and Randy entered the house.

Zilas had twenty-dollar bills scattered on the kitchen and bedroom floors.

"This man has really lost his mind, leaving all this money on the floor. You'd better pick it up and use it." Randy laughed hysterically. "I don't care how much witchcraft he practices. Money is money, girl."

As they went farther into the house, they saw that the altar and the other contents of Zilas's ritual were still in place. Kanasia told Randy that she wasn't staying there for now. She didn't trust Zilas. Randy dropped her back off at Paris's. The girls were playing with Paris's two daughters, Sophia and Stella, and her son, Simon, who was the same age as Charlotte. Samantha was watching the soaps on TV in the bedroom. They had been living with Paris for two weeks now. It was amazing how Shannon and Charlotte adapted to being away from home and their father.

But her mother wasn't enjoying it, because she was missing her room, her phone calls to her friends, and the ability to feel comfortable in her own home. She knew that Kanasia had to get them back to some type of normalcy, as this was destroying their family like crazy. It was four days until Charlotte's second birthday, and she had not planned anything for her, because of all the confusion. She decided to take some time off from work and keep the girls home too. She was afraid of what might happen to all of them, especially after having Zilas removed from the house. She found out through her friends that Zilas was living with one of his friends whose name was Hemmy. She didn't know what to do. She was afraid to go back into her own house, was afraid of her husband, and was also confused, depressed, and angry for having to go through all these changes.

She also had constant headaches and cried day and night. During the days, she was walking around like a zombie from lack of sleep. She would drive back by the house to see if it was still in one piece, and it was. Zilas had not burned it down as he promised, and she was so relieved.

She decided to go to the grocery store and get some groceries as well as go by the bakery to get Charlotte a birthday cake and ice cream. The whole house needed an uplift after all the drama they were experiencing, and a party seemed like just the thing to change the atmosphere in the house, placing everyone in a better mood.

The party did the trick. Everyone was laughing and enjoying the food and music. Little Charlotte ate every bite of her cake and had it all over her face, while Shannon laughed at her enjoying her cake. This scene made it seem that they didn't have a worry in the world.

Zilas never called or tried to contact her after she removed him from the house. In her heart, she was worried about him, but she was too fearful to contact him.

She took a week off work to try to get her head together and decide what she was going to do about her marriage and living situation. During this week, she made an appointment with Dr. Pellagrino and received an appointment within two days. During her appointment, she told Dr. Pellagrino all of the things she had been experiencing with Zilas, causing her loss of sleep and appetite; her nerves were terribly bad as well. Dr. Pellegrino ran another HIV test on her, also gave her prescriptions for her lack of appetite and anxiety.

She felt that she didn't want to go back to her house anymore. When she mentioned it to Paris, she encouraged her to go back home as soon as she felt up to it. "Your marriage is a good one. It was the AIDS that drove him to act like this," said Paris empathetically. "I don't think divorcing him is the answer. You and Zilas need counseling sessions and support group meetings. I'm going to call and find a support group for you and Zilas, "I'll go with you if you want me to", said Paris. I'm also going to call the hospital and speak to a social worker or doctor to find out why they never contacted you to tell you about the changes that Zilas was experiencing and why they never told you what to expect from him. This is so unfair to you all, but I'm going to get you the support you need so you can go back to your home without being afraid. There's no reason to leave him. You will lose your home and marriage, uprooting your whole family. You'll also have more difficulty starting over again."

When she returned to work the following week, there was a message left by one of the social workers at the clinic where Zilas went for his treatments. She returned the call and spoke to Ms. Garcia in social services. Ms. Garcia asked about Zilas and how things were working out with them and his illness. Ms. Garcia also told her that Zilas spoke to her about their living situation and that Zilas was staying with one of his friends from work.

"How's Zilas doing? Are there any changes with his condition?" she inquired of Ms. Garcia.

"I would like to have you come in so I can talk with you in person about Zilas," said Ms. Garcia. She made an appointment to meet with Ms. Garcia the following week.

As she hung up the telephone, she began to think about her situation and how Zilas's condition was an act of desperation to save his life. She began to think about the things she and Zilas accomplished together and how others were jealous of their marriage and accomplishments. She decided to call Zilas at his friend's house to see how he was doing. The phone rang twice, and then Zilas answered with episodes of continuous coughing and gagging. As the coughing continued, she began to feel bad about their separation and all the events that took place over the last month. She knew their continued separation would jeopardize Zilas's health even more.

After Zilas cleared his throat, he began to speak. "I missed out on Charlotte's second birthday, and that's not fair," he wept. "I'm not comfortable at Hemmy's house, and I know you all are not comfortable at your sister's home either." His tone was so sad.

Kanasia told Zilas that they should see what they could do to resolve all these issues they were having. She and Zilas agreed to meet at four o'clock at the Burger King near Paris's house, a more neutral atmosphere. She let Paris and her boyfriend, Kenny, know that she and Zilas made plans to meet up, but Kenny and Paris did not want her to go by herself to meet Zilas. They were both afraid for her to be with Zilas by herself. So Kenny went with her to Burger King, but he stayed outside, patrolling the parking lot and watching every move Zilas made inside the restaurant. Zilas was no idiot, and he immediately recognized Kenny watching him from outside the restaurant.

Zilas began to tell her that he felt bad about everything and did not like how the police threw him out of his house and that he was now under surveillance by Kenny.

"Zilas, you were out of control—the threats to destroy the house, the constant harassment at work, changing the locks on our home on me, the smoke-filled house, causing your whole family to relocate. Must I go on!" she yelled at Zilas. "You have done a lot of crazy things and jeopardized our lives. *I am afraid of you!*"

"I would never do anything to hurt you, your mother, or the girls," said Zilas. "I love you with all my heart, and I'm just afraid of losing you and the girls."

As they sat and talked, her fear of Zilas began to lift and she began to remember how much she loved him and wanted them to be back together again. But she told Zilas that they had to do things differently this time. "I want us to go for counseling and go to one of the support groups for HIV/AIDS and start going to church," she expressed to Zilas in a stern voice. "But most of all, Zilas, you have to tell your family, especially your mother, what's wrong with you. And *no more* white witchcraft or visiting that Dr. Diaz. If you can't do these things, I'm not coming back home with you. I need you to work with me and tell me what's going on and how you are feeling. No more not talking and sitting in the house staring at everyone as if you're in a trance! I can't live with you like this, Zilas."

Zilas agreed, and she reached into her pocket and gave him back the keys to their home. "When will you and girls be back home?" Zilas asked.

"It's late now, so I'll come back home tomorrow with the girls and my mother." They hugged, and Zilas thanked her for allowing him another chance. Zilas left the restaurant to return to home, and she went back to Paris's home with Kenny.

When she arrived at Paris's home, she had a discussion with Paris, Kenny, and her mother, letting them know that she had decided to return home the next day. She asked Paris if she thought she was doing the right thing.

"You should be okay as long as Zilas gets counseling and both of you join some support group."

"I'm happy to be going home," said her mother in an excited, relieved voice.

She ran to let Shannon and Charlotte know that the next morning we would be going back home to Daddy. They were excited and started jumping for joy. She began to pack their clothes, and the next morning she loaded up the car.

She thanked and hugged Paris, Kenny, and the children, and they began to drive back to their home.

It was the weekend, and they were moving back home with Zilas. About 30 percent of her was happy, but the other 70 percent of her was afraid of what to expect from him. She wanted to believe that he would change for the better and not practice witchcraft, but doubt was crawling up her spine. So to start the reunion back off on a positive note, she had her cousin Jay, who was a minister, come over to the house to pray throughout each room and bless it. This made both her and her mother feel much more comfortable in their home.

However, throughout all the happiness that Zilas displayed in having them back home together as a family, she still felt fear of the unknown, visualizing the clouds of billowing smoke plummeting throughout the house, accompanied with the aroma of scorching surfaces. She cried to God, asking him, "Why do I have to go through this pain and fear?"

She suffered from insomnia the first few nights back at home as well, and the scene of all the horrible events that occurred with Zilas haunted her day and night. She began to pray more and read her Bible, asking God for his protection and guidance in her life as well as for her family. Despite all of Zilas's desperate lifesaving attempts, she knew in her heart that before this HIV/AIDS thing, she and Zilas had a great marriage consisting of great conversations. He was a good husband, provider, father, supporter, and sex partner. He was fun, friendly, trusting, and cared for her mother as if she were his own. She knew that if anything ever were to happen to him that she would never find a man to equal up to his love, compassion, generosity, and good heart that he displayed earlier in their relationship. These were the qualities that made her fall in love with him, and he was her rescuer in her time of need during those horrible years of family abuse and neglect administered by her brothers.

18

~~~

The next week began, and they were ready to get back into their routine, accompanied with a counseling session and a group support meeting for AIDS patients and their families. Paris accompanied them to their first support group meeting via the Hyacinth AIDS Foundation at a church near her home. This support group was predominately white, and they were the only people of color there.

It was a surreal experience listening to the other AIDS patients talk about their experiences with their medical treatments and medications as well as how they coped with family, friends, and life in general. Zilas's face looked sad as he watched and listened to them. Some of them looked as if they were going to die any day, with their skin being so pale, bones protruding out of their clothes, hair so thin and resembling that fine soft curl of newborn babies' hair, bodies so weak they couldn't even walk anymore and were using wheelchairs or walkers to get around. It was quite depressing looking at those patients and realizing that one day Zilas would be in the same position they were in. But the one thing that really amazed her was how humble they were, with the friendly, loving support and empathy of their families.

They attended other sessions at the hospital where Zilas had his treatments, which was located in the heart of Newark, in the black and Hispanic community. These meetings were different from the first ones because there was a lack of empathy. They were also able to participate in a group support meeting and listen to other families and how they coped with their loved ones that had HIV /AIDS. One particular family would not let their infected daughter even stay in the same part of the house with them. She was given an attic apartment and was not allowed to touch or hug them. She couldn't even eat with them or on the same plates, cups, or eating utensils. Kanasia's heart went out to her for being isolated and discriminated by the people she loved, her family. The worst part was that her own mother admitted to her that she was afraid to touch her for fear of contracting AIDS. They were blaming their family members for contracting the disease, and they showed no mercy. She felt that they were cold, for surely no one asks to get sick or wants to die. She always felt that everyone deserves love and if you can't get it from your family, then from whom? She never discriminated against Zilas, and she treated him with respect and love.

As the week advanced, Zilas's cough was constant. She could tell he wasn't feeling well. He began to sleep more and eat less, so he went to visit his doctor at the clinic and was admitted the same day for further observation. After the doctor ran tests, he discovered Zilas had pneumonia again. Zilas remained in the hospital for three weeks. She hated to see Zilas go in the hospital, but she felt safer with him in than without. Her comfort zone was finally restored, and she was able to get back into her routine at home with the girls and her mother.

During Zilas's hospitalization, he realized that she was a good wife and that she tolerated him because of her love for him. He called her one night from his hospital room, apologizing for his past actions, conveying that he would never do anything to hurt her or jeopardize their family. Zilas was flirting with her too and said, "Honey, I love those Chinese eyes of yours; you are beautiful!" Zilas confessed that he overheard some of his male coworkers talking about her, saying that she was hot and sexy but they would be afraid to touch her with a ten-foot pole because of her husband's illness. Zilas apologized for subjecting her to such rejection, discrimination, and embarrassment. She was astonished how Zilas sounded like that Zilas she first met when she was seventeen, and she was falling in love with him all over again.

On Memorial Day 1989 and the doctor discharged Zilas from the hospital. She had planned a day out with the girls, consisting of a barbecue and watching *The Oprah Winfrey Show*. But after this hospitalization, Zilas became more demanding, didn't want to let her out of his sight, and it was as if she had a third child in the house. He followed her around the house from room to room. He would cuddle and hug her even as she listened to music or was lying in bed or sitting on the sofa. She was trying to understand his needs, knew that he was afraid of losing her, dying, and what he might be feeling, but it was unbearable at times. It was as if he was imposing on her leisure time, and she needed some type of positive outlet to relieve the new invasion that she was experiencing. She decided to join the gym. It was great to go to work because she felt free there and trapped at home.

When Kanasia felt that maybe all the trouble with Zilas and her was behind them, they planned a trip in July to St. Lucia, where his family resided. Before their trip, Zilas began becoming more obsessed with her. She found out through one of her friends that Zilas was paying two of her staff members to follow her and report her actions and whereabouts to him. She became very cautious of him and didn't let on as far as what she knew about his spies. She would even make up things deliberately so they could go back and tell him. She felt she was living with a psychopath, as he even talked to himself around the house.

Shannon told her mother that when she went to the store, her daddy told her, "Your mother isn't coming back home." He said that she was going to die and asked who they wanted to live with if something happened to their mother. "Which grandmother do you want to live with?" he asked Shannon and Charlotte.

The girls were frightened of Zilas, and Shannon said to Kanasia, "Mommy, we need to get away from Daddy!"

She gave both of them a hug. "We have to pray hard and believe God will protect us from all hurt, harm, and danger," she sweetly told her girls in a calm and loving voice. "We also need to pray that our home will become peaceful again so we can live without fear."

They all continued to pray, but Zilas began to back away from prayer and was on his own agenda, and their attending support meetings stopped also. Her nerves were once again on a roller coaster, with her weight dropping, insomnia, and crying in the basement or kitchen when Zilas would give her room to breathe. There were days when she would just break down and cry even if someone shared a joke with her. Her reactions were so twisted and crossed, like wires connected to the wrong prong on a motherboard of a computer.

Four days before their trip to St. Lucia, Charlotte's eye became swollen from an insect bite, so Zilas took her to the doctor to be examined, also bringing Shannon along, and while he was there, he began to have chest pains. The doctor's office called 911 to have Zilas taken to the hospital and notified Kanasia's mother about Zilas. Kanasia had been out shopping for their trip to St. Lucia, and when she arrived home, her mother told her that Zilas was on his way to the hospital that was across the street from her cousin Jaye's house, adding that the girls were with him in the ambulance. Her mother called Jaye to ask him to pick up the girls from the hospital and bring them home, telling him that Kanasia was on her way up to the hospital.

She raced up to the emergency room and found Zilas on a stretcher with oxygen and a cardiac monitor. He was crying as soon as she entered the room, and her heart went out to him. The cardiologist at the hospital wanted to admit him, but Zilas refused to be admitted. "I have to go home to St. Lucia to see my sick mother," said sobbing Zilas.

"Mr. Drummond, you're sick too, and this time it's your irregular heartbeat. It's not safe for you to travel," stated the doctor. But Zilas was determined to go see his mother. The doctor treated him with medication, gave him a referral to see a cardiologist once he returned from St.Lucia, and discharged him. As Kanasia took him home, she instructed him that she did not want him to drive his car anytime soon.

Soon they were only hours away from leaving for St. Lucia, and her mood was not feeling this trip at all. But she knew that if she refused, there would be hell from Zilas. She felt it was a mercy mission.

They had reservations for two weeks, but she told him she could only stay for one week because of work. Zilas wasn't happy about this and wanted her to stay the whole two weeks. But she made arrangements with the airlines once they arrived in St. Lucia to go back home with the girls within a week. She felt this would give her a break from dealing with his sickness and madness, plus he could spend time with his family.

While she was on the telephone with the airlines, the representative told her the change had already been made by her husband for the four of them to return to Illinois in a week instead of two. She was livid with him for being so sneaky and trying to be vindictive. Moreover, in the midst of his spiteful rampage, he forgot to take along his cardiac medication that the doctor prescribed at the emergency room. He told her that he forgot it but that he would be okay without it.

When they arrived at his mother's house, hugs were overflowing and Zilas's mood transformed into that loving, caring man she once knew. He took her out on the town for drinks and to his favorite burger joint. She put the last episode of his evilness behind her and decided to have a good time, and they did. He also showed her around St. Lucia and took her to his favorite restaurants and clubs he used to frequent. They didn't stay out long that night so that Zilas could get some rest since they'd had such an active day and night.

At five o'clock in the morning, Zilas woke up complaining of chest pain, and he was sweating profusely. Kanasia jumped out of bed and ran to her brother-in law's room to tell him that they needed him to take them to the emergency room at the nearest hospital right away. They rushed Zilas to the hospital. As she looked at Zilas, she noticed the tears running down his face as he panted for breath. He was as pale as an albino person.

Once they arrived in the emergency room, Zilas was transported to the treatment room via stretcher. Within minutes, the staff placed him on oxygen, heart and blood pressure monitors, and an oxygen saturation monitor. Zilas wept while his mother comforted him and held his hand. The doctor came in the room to examine him and gave orders for the nurse to draw his blood to find out what was going on with his electrolytes and cardiac enzymes to see if he had had a heart attack. They consistently conducted a tracing of his heart rhythm via the heart monitor.

After a few hours of observation, the doctor returned to inform them that Zilas's heart rate was so fast because in the lower chambers of his heart, the ventricles were contracting prematurely, causing the chest pain, low blood pressure, and fast heart rate. Kanasia told the doctor that the same thing happened in Illinois a day before they arrived in St. Lucia and that they gave Zilas medication to treat it but Zilas forgot it at home.

The emergency room doctor said, "Mr. Drummond, I recommend you return to Illinois and see the cardiologist as soon as possible! It's not medically safe for you to stay here with these new symptoms. You also need a blood transfusion, and you should return to your regular doctors for continued care." The doctor gave them a letter for the airlines to arrange an emergency flight home for all of them the next day, and they held Zilas until he was stable and pain-free. Once Zilas was discharged from the hospital, they went back to his mother's home and she contacted the airlines. She had success, and they were able to schedule their flight for Wednesday afternoon without any resistance. This was the worst trip of Kanasia's life because she believed if they didn't get him to the hospital on time, Zilas may have died over in St. Lucia. Was that his wish, to die where he once lived, near his family?

Zilas's family was very scared and nervous for him, and they finally started to give her the respect and appreciation she deserved. His cousins came to visit him, and Zilas looked so happy to see them. He hugged them and laughed with them. This was a bittersweet feeling because she knew this would probably be the last time he saw them. While they were laughing, she was crying, and his brother, Reginald, came in to console her. He told her that he wanted to come back with them to Illinois, but due to his finances, he could only accompany them to Puerto Rico to catch their connecting flight. Reginald asked his mother if she wanted to come back with them to Illinois. She stated, "I can't handle Zilas being sick!"

Kanasia became furious and blurted out, "She's his mother! How does she think I deal with it and I'm only twenty-four years old? I've had sleepless nights, weight loss, headaches, anxiety attacks, a constant upset stomach, and near nervous breakdowns! I carried this burden of not telling his family due to his wishes for two years, not to mention worrying about my daughters and myself becoming infected too!"

There was silence in the room, not even a whisper. She felt that the only reason they now appreciated her was because they were afraid and didn't want to deal with Zilas's illness. She discontinued the conversation and went into the room with the girls to prepare to leave the next afternoon and get some sleep.

Finally their travel day back to Illinois arrived, and Kanasia packed all their clothes, so anxious to return home. Zilas's family accompanied them to the airport, and as they arrived, the airline's security personnel met them at the gate with a wheelchair for Zilas. They said their good-byes to the family and boarded their flight to Puerto Rico and then to their connecting flight for Illinois. As they travelled, Zilas was fine, without any reoccurrences of chest pain or shortness of breath.

They finally arrived in Illinois and took a cab back to the house. As soon as she opened the door, the girls began to run all over the house as if just released from prison. Zilas also had a look of relief as well due to being back home, where he was safe and could receive better medical attention. She helped Zilas settle in and then went into her mother's room to tell her about their horrible trip to St. Lucia. She too was happy that they were back safely.

Kanasia and Zilas still had another week left of vacation time, and they decided to take him back to the doctor for a follow-up visit and let him know of Zilas's episode of chest pain and shortness of breath in St. Lucia. The doctor recommended that they schedule an appointment with a cardiologist to see what was going on with Zilas's heart. They were able to get an appointment that Wednesday with a cardiologist that the hospital recommended.

The cardiologist ran every cardiac test possible but was unable to find anything wrong with Zilas's heart, so they returned home to relax during their last few days of vacation. Things were pretty relaxed on the home front, so Kanasia decided to ask Zilas if he had any objections to her going out for a few hours on Friday with her friend Jane. "No, honey, I don't mind," Zilas responded. However, deep down inside, she knew Zilas really did mind. He hated to see her relax or go out.

On Friday, everything at home was fine and pleasant until she started getting dressed to go out with Jane. Zilas's facial expression changed from pleasant to a look of glowing jealousy with anger flowing from his eyes. She went to inform her mother that she was going out with Jane and kissed her good-bye. She left to pick up Jane, and they headed to a club to dance. When they arrived at the club, it was so packed that there wasn't anywhere to sit except at the bar. The music was hot, and the dance floor was so full that you couldn't even see the floor.

"What can I get for you ladies tonight?" asked the bartender.

"Two sex on the beach, please," Kanasia called back to the bartender through the music and surrounding conversations. She started to relax, and she and

Jane talked and drank a couple of more rounds. Time was flying, and as she consumed her drinks, she began to relax even more, to the point where she was forgetting all about Zilas and his recent problems. Then she started mixing her drinks and decided to have her favorite drink, a kamikaze. Wow, now she felt like dancing the night away.

She was accompanied to the dance floor by a handsome guy, and then she saw Jane with a young man. They joined them. They danced until it was time for the club to close, and as she approached the parking lot, she felt as if her head were in a washing machine on the spin cycle—then her stomach was twirling too. She was so intoxicated that she couldn't see right either, and the bad part was that Jane didn't know how to drive. They sat in the car in the parking lot as Kanasia expelled all the beverages out of her system. Unfortunately, she threw up all over her dress and the car floor. It took over an hour until she began to sober up.

Jane was helpful and encouraged her to focus on Zilas, which was what got them back to her house in one piece. However, as soon as she arrived, she ran to her bathroom to throw up continuously. Jane was afraid to let her go home like this so she let her lie down on her sofa to sleep for a while until she sobered up. She went to sleep and woke up at six the next morning. She felt much better but still tipsy.

"Jane, I'm ready to go home now. Thank you for everything," she said.

"You' re welcome, Kanasia, but I'm not comfortable with you driving yourself. I'm going to call a cab for us and let my boyfriend, Carl, drive your car and follow the cab," said Jane in a concerned voice.

She agreed, and a cab arrived to take her home, with Carl following in her car. But the cab was going fast, and she soon noticed that Carl was not right behind them on the road. Therefore, they arrived at the house before Carl did. The cab driver said he'd wait for Carl to arrive, and Kanasia began to walk toward her house, not realizing her house keys weren't available because Carl had them. She rang the doorbell to get in, and by this time, Carl pulled up in front of the house in the car.

Zilas was in the house watching from the living room window, and as he answered the door, he was furious with her. "Where the hell is my car, Kanasia, and who are you letting drive it!" he yelled. He'd awakened the girls and had them sitting in the living room waiting up for her. Zilas followed her in the house after she went to get her keys from Carl, and he was cursing her out and screaming at her. Then the next thing she knew, as she was walking up the stairs to use the bathroom, Zilas threw his wineglass at her head.

The girls began to cry hysterically, and her mother screamed, "Zilas, Zilas, please stop it!" She ran so fast up the stairs, ducking the flying glass and still feeling intoxicated. Zilas's face was red, his eyes were red and dilated, hair was protruding from his scalp, and his mouth was expelling words of anger. Then he abruptly went to inspect his car, and as he walked out of the house, he was cursing her out for allowing another man to drive his car. Then she could hear him screaming about her getting sick in his car.

Kanasia went back down to get the girls to make sure they were okay and put them in their rooms. "Daddy kept saying you weren't coming back home," cried Shannon.

She picked up Shannon, hugging and comforting her, letting them know that she was there and that everything would be okay. She reached over to pick up Charlotte as well, also hugging and kissing her. She put them to bed and went into her mother's room. Samantha told her that Zilas had been drinking all night while she was out and was acting crazy. As she went to the bathroom to run her bathwater, she began to feel worse physically, so she hurried and took a bath and put on her nightgown so she could lie down to rest.

While she was resting, Paris called and told her mother that Zilas arrived at her home at seven that morning, telling her that she went out with Jane and accusing her of being so high on cocaine and drunk from alcohol that she messed up his car and let another man drive her home. He let Paris look inside the car, still complaining about her going out. Paris said that Zilas was so mad, also accusing her of taking money out of her savings account to give to Jane so she could buy her cocaine.

After Kanasia woke and her mother told her about Zilas's latest rampage, she called his brother and insisted they talk to him so he could calm down. She informed them that she was in no shape to drive home so her friend and her boyfriend were looking out for her safety. "Zilas should be happy that she arrived home safely and not go around starting trouble by spreading vicious rumors about her," she angrily stated to his brother. "I love Zilas, but I am not going to tolerating his craziness!" Zilas's brother told her that he would come over later to speak to him.

Once Zilas found this out, his rage increased. He began monitoring her telephone calls by picking up the telephone extension in the house when someone called for her, listening in the background. When Jane called, Zilas yelled at her, "Never call or visit my house again. You've caused a disturbance in my house and relationship!" Jane listened to Zilas, and she apologized to her for his behavior as she ended the call.

Zilas was like a storm in progress, on a mission to pay back anyone that caused their family problems or discriminated against them. He began causing problems by exposing those involved in extramarital affairs, those were selling drugs throughout the hospital, and those who brought weapons to the job. Whatever bad information he had on employees of the hospital was brought to the human resource department.

Kanasia was becoming more fearful, frustrated, and tired of living with Zilas and dealing with all the behavioral changes. She just wanted to take her girls and her mother and leave for good. She couldn't sleep or eat again. This led her to pray and read her Bible on a regular basis.

19

It was now November of 1989, and Zilas was having more complications, like low blood pressure, fever, and chest pains. He also needed a blood transfusion, so his doctor admitted him into the hospital to treat him. Zilas had a difficult time breaking the fever, and what they thought would be a couple of days turned into three weeks.

The night before Thanksgiving, Kanasia began to prepare a nice holiday meal. As she was putting the seasoned turkey in the oven the next morning, the phone rang. It was Zilas, saying that he was coming home. He had decided to sign himself out of the hospital against medical advice.

A short while later, she watched as Zilas arrived with his friend Fred, whom he'd apparently called to drop him off at the house. She watched Zilas as he got out of the car, and she could tell by his slow movements and panting breath that he didn't feel well at all. Zilas walked into the house and went straight to the bathroom. He was incoherent and muttering that he was having a difficult time urinating. She told him that he needed to go back to the hospital, adding that his breathing was horrible. She couldn't understand anything he was saying, and it sounded as if he were swimming underwater. With every word, there was gurgling, and she could see his weakness as he walked. "I'm not going back to that St. Michael's," Zilas said in a muffled voice.

"Okay, Zilas, but you *are* going to another hospital now," Kanasia said in a stern voice. She took the turkey out of the oven, and she and the girls took Zilas to Beth Israel Medical Center. As they went into the emergency waiting area, Zilas was taken in right away and placed on a heart monitor and oxygen. Blood was drawn for lab work. She informed the nurses that she was going to drop the girls back off at home with her mother and that she would return. Once she arrived at home, she began to make the girls and her mother ham and cheese sandwiches and poured them some fruit punch. She helped the girls settle in and then headed back to the hospital to see what was going on with Zilas.

As Kanasia was driving, she thought what an awful Thanksgiving it was. While others were enjoying it, eating festive dishes, joking around, and having fun, her family was eating ham and cheese sandwiches and she was running back up to the hospital.

Once she reached the emergency room, the doctors came in to tell her that Zilas was in pulmonary edema, which caused his lack of urination and respiratory distress. "We're going to transfer Mr. Drummond to ICU as soon as possible to intubate him," said Dr. Jones. Kanasia looked into Zilas's eyes as tears of fear rolled down his cheeks.

Once Zilas reached the ICU unit, the nurses told Kanasia that she had to leave while they placed him in an induced coma to alleviate his breathing issues. She left the ICU but stayed in the waiting room for hours, tearful and full of fear. Zilas was still unstable even after he was intubated, and she went back in to see him and hold his hand. She was glad she'd insisted on bringing him to the hospital. The doctors told her that Zilas was drowning in his own fluids.

She left the hospital to go home to get some rest but in the process decided to call Zilas's mother to let her know his status. His mother abruptly told her that she was mailing some papers for Zilas to sign and that she should make sure he signed them and mailed them back to her. Kanasia became furious with her and told her she should be ashamed of herself for being so cold and unsympathetic. She told her, "I am not having him sign anything, nor can he sign it anyway!" She slammed down the phone.

Zilas's mother showed up at the hospital two weeks later, bringing the paperwork with her. Zilas was now out of ICU, but he was very quiet and not eating. He also looked depressed. His mother was so afraid she was going to be contaminated that she sat about ten feet away from him. It was so uncomfortable for Kanasia to be around her, so she left the room in intervals. During the last interval, his mother followed her into the hall, trying to provoke her into an argument.

"Keep away from me and my family!" Kanasia yelled at her. She became so angry that she wanted to hit her, and as she walked away, his mother continued to follow her. Finally the nurses told them that if they didn't keep the noise down, they would have to leave the premises. So she decided to leave and let Zilas's family visit alone with him.

20

As the Christmas season approached, Zilas was still in the hospital. He was getting stronger physically but was so depressed. He didn't even call Kanasia anymore at home. She decided to take a few days off from visiting Zilas so she could get some sleep and give the girls and her mother some quality time. While at home, she and the girls decorated the house, picked up a live Christmas tree, and placed gifts under the tree. When she and the girls went to visit Zilas, he was so happy and said, "I miss you and the girls!"

On December 23, 1989, Zilas was finally discharged from the hospital. When he arrived home, he was weak and went straight to the bedroom to lie down. There he spent much of the evening speechless, lying down or staring at the floor. Christmas Eve rolled in, and the girls were so excited about opening their gifts during their midnight ritual. Kanasia was so happy that Zilas was home for the holidays with them.

As midnight approached, they began to prepare to celebrate Christmas as a family, gathered in the living room around the tree. She encouraged Zilas to join her mother, the girls, and her downstairs, but he refused. He continued sitting on the side of the bed, staring at the floor. She felt so bad for him, but at the same time, she had to keep up a good front for the girls' sakes. She didn't want anything to ruin their Christmas, especially after all the miserable times they'd endured. Therefore, since Zilas refused to come to the living room, she and the girls took his gifts to the bedroom. He was so tearful and apologetic because this was the first time he was unable to buy them gifts. Kanasia told him in a loving voice, "We understand, honey. You were in the hospital!" She hugged him.

The girls surrounded them, their voices filled with joy as they repeated, "Daddy, Daddy, look what Santa brought me for Christmas!" This uplifted his spirits, and he began to talk more, even smiling occasionally. On Christmas Day, they were showered with calls from relatives and friends.

Just as quickly as Christmas had arrived, New Year's Eve approached. This was one of their favorite holidays of the year because it meant a fresh start. It was on a Sunday this year, so they went to morning service at church. When they returned, Kanasia cleaned the house and cooked. She began to make such hors d'oeuvres as shrimp cocktails, codfish fritters, and pigs in blankets. She had bought champagne to toast in the New Year of 1990.

As the night grew late, they put the television on to watch Dick Clark's New Year's Eve show, waiting for the countdown and for the ball to drop. As the countdown began, all but Zilas began to scream out the numbers in excitement. "Happy New Year!" they exclaimed. The girls were running around the house in joy. She had to chase them down to hug them. She gave her mother a kiss on the cheek and then turned to her husband and placed a big kiss on his cheek.

As he looked at the television, Zilas suddenly asked, "What's going on?" She felt so bad that he didn't even realize it was the celebration of a new year. She sat beside him, looking into his beautiful hazel eyes, and said, "Honey, it's New Year nineteen ninety!" She kissed him again on his cheek, holding his hand tightly, and as her lips left his face, she realized that that might be their last New Year together. All of a sudden, tears uncontrollably ran from her eyes to her cheeks, and she ran quickly to the bathroom to avoid having him see her cry.

January 1990 was peaceful. The fear for the safety of her and her family's lives was gone. The constant fighting with Zilas was over. However, he was unable to return to work due to his weakness and visual changes, and now his mind was going. He was always hallucinating and talking to himself, floors, walls, and ceilings, also seeing people in their bedroom carrying on conversations. Kanasia would try to redirect him when he started doing this, but it didn't always work.

21

⁓ ℳ ⁓

During the month of February 1990, Zilas was becoming worse physically and mentally. He was hospitalized once again for chest pains and his altered mental status, and it was discovered by the doctor that he needed a blood transfusion too. Zilas remained in the hospital for three weeks, but this hospitalization was different from the others. One of the house doctors called Kanasia at home one night to ask how she felt about putting a DNR code on Zilas's chart. "DNR is for do not resuscitate." He went on to state, "Zilas isn't getting any better. He's very ill and suffering, and at this point, there's nothing else we can do for your husband." She began to cry hysterically, feeling that just talking about a DNR meant she was assisting in Zilas's death. The doctor ended the call by asking her to think about it and to let him know so they could place it on his chart.

She was so upset over the conversation that she didn't even go to work the next day. She called her supervisor and told her that she was not in any shape mentally to work. Take all the time you need. I understand," replied Lolita. So she took the day off, but she couldn't get the conversation with the doctor out of her mind. She'd known Zilas was bad but was in denial about the end of his life. She was tired of seeing him suffer, the discrimination they endured as a family, and all the mental changes. Deep inside, she knew there was no recovery—the doctor was right—but giving up on Zilas and enforcing a death code was not an easy decision either. She decided to ignore the doctor's advice about the DNR, and she went on with her daily routine of visiting Zilas at the hospital.

Zilas was discharged from the hospital two weeks later, but back at home, he was deteriorating rapidly, both mentally and physically. He was overcome by weakness, and now it was as if Kanasia were talking care of another child. He only left the bedroom to go to the bathroom. She left his meals on the nightstand by the bed before she left for work each day. Sometimes she came back home and saw that the food was never touched. She took care of him the best she could and even had friends of theirs come over to the house to stay with him when she had to go out. Zilas could no longer be left unattended due to all the changes he was experiencing.

When she came home from work, she would run into the bedroom to check on him, crawl into the bed next to him, and cradle him tightly. He welcomed it and held her close but never spoke. As she was holding him one night, she could tell he was in pain, and he also felt hot. "Zilas, what's hurting, honey?" It took a few minutes, and then he said, "My chest, my chest!" Tears were streaming down his face.

She told him, "Honey, we need to go to the hospital to get help!" She left Zilas to go to her mother's room to tell her she was going to take him to the hospital. She got Zilas ready, and they left for the emergency room again. It was so crowded, but they still took Zilas into the treatment area and began taking his vital signs, drawing blood, and giving him oxygen. The nurses told her that he would be admitted; however, it would be a few days before he was issued a room because they were overcrowded.

Kanasia stayed with Zilas for a few hours, and then she kissed him and told him she needed to go back home and check on the girls. She left her contact information with the nurses and asked them for the telephone number so she could check on Zilas to see if he received a room before she returned to the hospital. The nurse gave her the telephone number, and she left for home.

When she arrived home, she went straight into her bedroom, lying down on the bed and sobbing about all the decisions she needed to make in reference to Zilas. He could no longer be accountable for anything due to his failing health, both mentally and physically. She felt so alone and helpless, not knowing where to turn for help or an impartial understanding ear.

The phone rang. "I'd like to speak to Mrs. Drummond," said the caller. "This is Dr. Rison at Beth Israel Medical Center."

"This is she, but is everything okay with my husband?"

"No, your husband needs to be intubated and placed on a respirator because he fell into pulmonary edema along with pneumonia," replied Dr. Rison.

Kanasia began to shake like a swaying tree, with her heart pounding that steady single beat. "Okay, but when will he be placed in a room?"

"We're transferring him to ICU now so that we can monitor him more closely," said Dr. Rison.

"Okay, I'm on my way up to the hospital to see my husband, and hopefully I'll see you once I arrive."

"Yes, Mrs. Drummond. I'll be in ICU until he is stabilized. See you soon."

Kanasia arrived at the hospital and was able to see Zilas after his intubation. Water flowed from her eyes as she watched Zilas in a medically induced coma, watching him struggle to breathe, his chest rising and falling so rapidly and labored even after being placed on a respirator. This scene was driving her crazy, and she knew it was getting to a point where one day his struggling for air would be over.

As she held Zilas's hand and began to pray, a housekeeper entered the room to clean. "Hello, ma'am. Don't worry—he's going to be okay. He's young. Keep praying!"

She looked into her eyes with such sorrow and replied, "Thank you!"

She decided to leave the room to take a break, and as she approached the hall, Dr. Rison was entering Zilas's room. She ran back to see what Dr. Rison had to say about Zilas's condition.

"Mrs. Drummond, Zilas is not getting any better. He's having a difficult time breathing on his own. We're going to keep him on the respirator and monitor his labs and arterial blood gases to see where his breathing status is. Hopefully he'll recover soon. But have you considered making him a DNR?"

Oh no, here we go again. She was trying to avoid this like crazy. "I've thought about it, but at this time, I'm unable to make that decision, Dr. Rison."

"Okay, Mrs. Drummond. I don't want to put pressure on you, but there really isn't much more we can do for your husband medically. Even if he is revived during a code, his quality of life is decreasing. I just want you to understand what we are facing going forward with his health."

"Well, I'll let you know what I decide, Doctor," she replied.

After a few weeks passed, Zilas was weaned off the respirator and transferred to a step-down unit from ICU. Zilas was so quiet now, barely spoke, and was always in a staring mode whenever Kanasia saw him. She continued her regular routine of visiting him at the hospital, but she tried to take the girls out in the afternoons to break free of the sadness she was feeling. The park became their haven for happiness and escape. As she sat in the park and watched the girls play one day, her mind went back to Zilas's condition. She knew she needed to make him a DNR as soon as possible to avoid all the unnecessary treatments, tests, and procedures that would not work for him at this point.

When she returned to the hospital the next day, she went to the nurses' station and requested to put a DNR code on Zilas's chart. The nurse contacted Dr. Rison, and he placed the DNR order in the chart. She walked away feeling as if she'd just put a gun to Zilas's head. Having to make this decision left her feeling guilty, as if she were giving up on Zilas. The only person she discussed her decision with was her mother because she felt that if she discussed it with Zilas's family, they would accuse her of trying to off him for the insurance money.

Within a few weeks, Zilas was discharged from the hospital. But this time Zilas was referred to a different clinic that was associated with Beth Israel. The dementia was worse now, and Zilas needed to be watched twenty-four hours a day. Kanasia stayed home to care for him. She took him back and forth for his checkups and his pentamidine treatments.

Zilas became worse. The infectious disease doctor at the clinic told Kanasia that the disease was affecting Zilas's brain, causing him to have encephalitis, and said that the pentamidine treatments were no longer working. "Mrs. Drummond, placing your husband in a nursing home would give him the twenty-four hour care he needs and also give you a break."

Kanasia became indignant with the doctor. "I am not putting my husband in any nursing home. He is not elderly or some animal that needs shelter! He's my husband, and I love him. We worked in nursing homes and know the lack of care he would receive, not to mention that he would die faster. No, thank you, Doctor, for your recommendation! How about you write an order to have a nurse and nurse's aide come into our home to care for him?" The doctor complied, writing an order for Zilas to receive home health care and also signing his papers so Zilas could apply for disability payments.

One good thing about Zilas being at this new clinic was that there was a therapist there for counseling for the patient or family. Kanasia took advantage of this and made an appointment to see her. Her name was Amoli Woods, and she was a psychotherapist who was thorough, direct, and helped Kanasia to make it through the rough times. They discussed the scenarios of Zilas not being around or her becoming HIV positive.

The therapist made her more aware of options for her situation, helped her to face the what-ifs, and most of all, helped her to realize that she was an incredible, phenomenal woman with the strength of a warrior. All of these things helped her to rebuild her self-esteem and develop better and more constructive coping mechanisms. She was able to care for her family better, understand the changes that Zilas had encountered throughout his illness, and accept the things that she could not change. She made sure she met with her once a week, keeping every appointment. This therapist was what she needed from the beginning, someone outside the picture to help her realize her potential and options, to voice her concerns or worries to, and most of all, someone to understand and not judge.

Kanasia was contacted by a home health agency RN, who came to their home to interview and assess Zilas. During the waiting process, Zilas grew worse, having difficulty seeing, walking, standing, eating, and drinking. As he was also incontinent, she began to buy him adult diapers to avoid a mess all over the bed or floors. Even Zilas's appearance was changing again; he resembled an elderly man with little hair. He was underweight, fragile, weak, and mindless. Zilas was approved for home health care after about three weeks, and she cared for Zilas until the home health aide service could start.

It was now April, and Kanasia's brother Rick came home for his military leave from Germany. She and Samantha were so happy to see him, and it was a good feeling for Kanasia to have one of her big brothers around for support. Rick was surprised to see Zilas in this condition since it had been seven years he saw him last.

Rick was so helpful. He washed the dishes; took care of their mom, Zilas, and the girls; and never discriminated against Zilas because of his AIDS.

It was also approaching Zilas's forty-second birthday. She didn't know what to get him, and he was so out of it mentally. She decided to cook him a nice dinner, buy a cake, and do a small celebration with just the family in the house. She sat next to Zilas on the bed, trying not to cry, and with a happy sounding voice, she shouted out, "Happy birthday, Zilas!" As she embraced him, he began to cry. She consoled him, held him tightly, and whispered how much she loved him.

The following week was her twenty-fifth birthday, and she was in no mood for celebrating, smiling, laughing, or talking. She felt as if she were swimming in misery. Little by little, she was losing control, going under, and drifting to the bottom of the ocean floor. She spent her birthday listening to music and lying down in bed next to Zilas. He turned to her and said in a low tone, "Honey, is it your birthday?"

"Yes," she replied.

Zilas reached over, kissed her on her cheek, and said, "Happy birthday!"

Two days after her birthday, on April 14, Zilas began to have more complications. He was unable to get up out of bed, and he began to develop fluid all over his body, accompanied with excessive shortness of breath. Kanasia decided she needed to take Zilas to the hospital immediately. Since he could no longer walk and was having a difficult time breathing even during a resting state, she called 911 to transport him to the emergency room. This was the first time she had ever called 911 for Zilas after all the years he was sick. Rick got the girls and Samantha settled, and they took off for the emergency room, following the ambulance. She was so nervous for Zilas, fearing that this could be it. Thoughts of losing her husband, her children's father, were all too real, uncontrollable, and happening very rapidly.

During this time, Zilas began to talk again to her; his spirits even seemed to be up. She kept up a good front and stayed calm, even though she was scared as hell. Once again the hospital was full, so Zilas stayed in the emergency room for a day and then was admitted to ICU to be intubated again for pulmonary edema. He got better within two weeks and was weaned off the ventilator and sent to the coronary care unit for monitoring.

After being extubated, Zilas was talking like a hurricane to everyone who came in contact with him. However, along with his talking came a fear like no other she'd witnessed before. Zilas began to cry out, "I'm going to die, and I don't want to, honey!" She hugged him, consoled him, and told him she was there for him. But she knew that an impending sense of doom was weighing on him heavily.

Zilas didn't sleep at night at the hospital, constantly crying and screaming, "I'm dying. Call my wife, please! I want my wife!" When she would leave the hospital to go home, Zilas's anxiety level grew worse and the nurses could not calm him down. Zilas would be so bad that she would have to return to the hospital and stay with him all night long. Thank God Rick was there so she didn't have to worry about leaving the girls and her mother alone. After she arrived, she would climb into bed with Zilas, hug him, pray, and read the Bible to him. Eventually, he would fall asleep in her arms.

After about two weeks, Zilas began to calm down, allowing her to return to work. Zilas was transferred from the CCU unit to a regular med-surg unit in the hospital. At this time, they were just monitoring him and keeping him comfortable. He became speechless again, and his eyes drifted off to another zone. He would look at Kanasia but never say a word, although there was a peaceful, calm look to his face.

She brought the girls and Rick up to the hospital to see him. The girls made pictures for him at the babysitter's and were so happy to hang them up in his room. Zilas watched as they hung them, and then they gave him a big group hug.

Spring brought great weather and days filled with bright sunshine. Little Charlotte's third birthday was approaching, so she took some time off to celebrate with her, Shannon, her mom, and Rick, ringing in her birthday with pizza, cake, and ice cream. It was such a nice day that while she was out buying the cake, she decided to buy some red roses to plant in the front of the house.

As Kanasia planted the roses, Shannon and Charlotte ran around from the front yard to the backyard, playing and having a great time in the sun. She had never planted flowers before, but it felt so great being outdoors, putting her energy and time into something positive and constructive. She discovered that this was another way to relieve her stress, take her mind off her problems, and feel good about herself.

The following day Rick wanted to go to the Woodbridge Mall, where their parents took them when they were younger. It was like a second home for them. After they shopped, they then went to eat at Red Lobster. She had a good time, and she currently had no worries.

To make sure Zilas was okay, she decided that she wanted to go see him before returning home. As they approached the patient information desk, the receptionist said that the doctor was trying to contact her to let her know that Zilas was transferred back into ICU for pulmonary edema. She and Rick rushed up the escalator to the ICU, searching for Zilas's nurse to get an update about his condition.

This time Zilas remained in the ICU from April 29 through May 2. He was then weaned from the ventilator and transferred back to a med-surg floor. Zilas was now stable, and his breathing was better, but he was silent consistently. He continued to stare at Kanasia, and she would hold his hand and pray with him each visit. There was an indescribable feeling of calmness and pain-free easy-breathing peacefulness in the air and on Zilas's face. Zilas's eyes were clear, and his complexion was glowing. There was no hint of sickness present. His hazel eyes were clear and so beautiful. He gazed at Kanasia as if he didn't want to stop looking at her, and he wasn't even blinking. As he stared at her, she was wondering what was going on in his mind. She held his hand and talked to him, but no words came out of his mouth.

She decided to go home. She gave Zilas a kiss on the cheek and told him she would see him tomorrow. But as she left, a funny feeling was riding her spirit; she couldn't shake it. She arrived at home as the weird feeling continued to overcome her, and she tried to take her mind off Zilas's face, but she couldn't. She began to weep uncontrollably, but she knew she had to keep her spirits up for the girls' sake. She had a burst of energy, so she cleaned the house, cooked, washed the girls' hair, and then gave both of them baths. She went to her mother's room as the girls were bathing to tell her how she was feeling. Samantha encouraged her to pray and read her Bible.

As she went back into the bathroom to get the girls out of the tub, the phone suddenly rang. Rick answered it, and Kanasia felt her heart begin to beat hard. Her anxiety level was off the radar. Who was calling this time of the night? Rick came to her. "It's the hospital, Kanasia," he said in a serious tone.

"Yes, this is Mrs. Drummond," she said into the receiver in a nervous voice.

"This is Dr. Williams, the house doctor, and I'm calling to tell you that Mr. Drummond passed away tonight."

She paused for about two minutes, and then she began to cry and scream hysterically, practically hyperventilating. "Why didn't anyone call me to tell me he was going to die?"

The doctor stated, "Mrs. Drummond, I'm calling you now."

"No, why didn't you call me when he began to have complications so I could be there with him! No one should die alone—and I wanted to be with him!"

Rick drove Kanasia to the hospital to see Zilas one last time before the funeral. As they arrived in his room, she couldn't believe Zilas was gone.

Zilas succumbed to AIDS and died on May 6, 1990, after suffering for three years with this disease.

May he rest in peace, and the love they shared forever be a part of their memories.

Good-bye, Zilas

Love, Kanasia, Shannon, Charlotte, and Samantha.

About the Author

Rachel Karrington is a registered nurse, mother, and a passionate advocate for connecting with one's spirituality and seeking mental health counseling during times of crisis. *Silence in a World Full of Thunder* is her debut novel.

Printed in the United States
By Bookmasters